Lying Doggo

An Eton Farce

By
Jan Needle

An old boy

(NB Jan Needle is a genuine old boy – just not of Eton)

SOME CRITICS

Brendan Gisby:
Roll over, Jonathan Swift – Jan Needle is kicking the political elite harder than you ever did!

It's not hard to work out who is being lampooned in this saucy yet sinister satire. It's all good dirty fun, but it also provides scarily accurate accounts of the workings of Eton, the very *raison d'être* of the place, and the over-privileged reptiles who infest it. Even scarier is the realisation that many of those reptiles will go on one day to enter politics and thence to take up positions in Government, from where they will run – and ruin – the country.

Bill Kirton:
For all its nasty truths, this is a pleasure to read.

'Revelling' is the wrong expression, because no-one can take any gratification from the fact that we've allowed this set of circumstances to persist for so long. I need time to suppress (although not reject) my anger and futility at these reminders of the system we've tolerated not only uncomplainingly but, by so many of our compatriots, encouragingly. A terrific job.

Mark Francois (who?):

'**Cummings is going** to come down there and sort you out his own way, and you won't like it'.

Marina Hyde:

Ooooooooooooooo!

Carole Cadwalladr:

In a world without consequences, the bad man will be king.

Professor Peter Thomson:

Will the reputation of Eton College survive, I wonder. Then I remember the habitual mendacity of the current occupant of 10 Downing Street and anticipate the spiral-spreading denials. Throaty guffaws.

Jan Needle has asserted his rights under the Copyright, Design and Patents Act, 1988, to be identified as the author of this work

©Jan Needle 2020

Cover: Jean Hobson ©2020

One

Gregor Goinn and Horus Nicholae de Peperpott Paste-Shippam started out at Eton on the same day. And both of them were rather lost.

Goinn was looking for his mater (as she'd told him to call her, for fear that he'd be bullied by the Badbobs), but if he found her, had to deny he knew her.

'Why, mum? Are you ashamed of me? You said yesterday I was worth two of any one of this lot.'

'That's as maybe. But you're of a different class.'

'What, from you? Does that mean that dad's not really my dad?'

'Pater, not dad. How many more times do I have to tell you? Of course he's your father, what do you take me for?'

'I'm just a bit confused, that's all. Sorry.'

'So shut up and listen. Pater went to grammar school, which makes him the scum of the earth. But if you learn nothing else in life, learn this: you never, ever, say sorry. Never apologise, and never, ever, ever explain. That's why I've got you into this school. It's their motto. The watchword that they live by. It's why they rule the world.'

'So pater went to grammar school but I'm never to tell anyone? Or apologise if they do find out?'

'They won't find out. And if they do, you tell them they are lying.'

'But that would be a lie.'

'You're catching on.'

'And lying's wrong.'

'Wrong. Getting caught is wrong. Telling the truth is for little people. The bigger the person, the bigger the lie. Think Donald Trump.'

'But Donald Trump's a crooked idiot.'

'And that's democracy. He is also, is he not, the President of the US of America, and thus the most powerful man in the history of the world. He says so himself. Would he tell a lie?'

'I can't imagine.'

'Which is why I've got you into this school (or School, as they call it) – so that you learn. Do you know how many Prime Ministers came here? Dozens. Including giants among men like Sir Anthony Eden and David Cameron. Have you ever heard of the Duke of Wellington?'

'Didn't he invent the rubber boot?'

'What about the battle of Waterloo? Have you heard

of that?'

'Named after the station? Trains to the Isle of Wight?'

'He was the British hero who said the battle of Waterloo was won on the playing fields of Eton. He beat Napoleon. The French emperor who invented brandy.'

'So they allow Frogs in this school do they? I thought it was meant to be posh.'

'It is – posh people have esoteric tastes. Wellington boasted it "stuck a poker slowly up my arse for four long years."'

'Gosh. You don't get that at comprehensive.'

'He also said he got a splendid education, which was worth the lifelong psychiatric bills. Then he seduced Napoleon's mistresses in Paris to show the superiority of the English system.'

'Mistresses? I've only heard of Josephine. She was black wasn't she?'

'She was creole, and she was his wife, not mistress. Napoleon divorced her because she didn't give him any boy children, and to show how much he missed her, he called the substitutes Josephine as well, all three of them. Then along comes Wellington and screws the lot. Power trip.'

'Weird. Almost as if he'd been to Eton himself.'

'He had.'

'But he was French!'

'Not Napoleon – the Duke of Wellington, idiot. In those days they didn't allow Johnny Foreigners into School, not even dictators. All changed now, of course. It's called the bottom line.'

'So they like blacks now, do they. What about girls?'

'Don't be silly. But blacks are okay if they're princes, kings and oil sheiks, or a combination of all four. It's not just the fees they bring, it's the gifts and scholarships they endow on top of their fifty grand a year. Some whitish foreigners are tolerated as well. Russians, for instance. It used to be a communist utopia so now it's owned by oligarchs, and run by that dead-eyed narcissist who's always got his tits out.'

'Are you saying Vlad Putin's gay? He's my hero.'

'Well he doesn't send his kids to Eton, does he? He says it's decadent. Oligarchs are respectable these days, even ex-communists, it says so on the tin. They're *straight*.'

'And talking about communists,' young Goinn said, 'why can't I admit I know you?'

'That's a *non sequitur*; your Latin's coming on a treat. And you don't know me because I'm not a dame yet, am I? Your dad went to grammar school, and I'm not a dame. I've got you in here, but you're not one of the chosen, and you never will be till I stop being a servant or your father gets a knighthood, which is distressingly unlikely in the scheme of things. I can't imagine what I ever saw in him.'

'How can you *ever* be a dame, though? You vote Labour.'

'Not that sort of dame, you stupid child,' she said. 'We're on a ladder, and we're going up. We're going to win.'

Through the doorway came a standard Eton bug, an archetype. Tall and plumpish, with a grin of vacuity that was almost monumental, a white silk shirt and floppy tie, and a tail-coat that was elegantly rumpled.

'I say,' he quacked. 'I say!'

'And here's the opposition,' said Mrs Goinn to her son. 'Mate in three moves I think.'

'You're in my chamber!' the apparition squeaked. 'I say! Oh gosh! Do you know who I am?'

Gregor Goinn glanced at his mater for some guidance, and took his cue from her. She stayed silent.

'I say! Dashed awkward, what? This is my room see, doncherknow? I mean I'm…well!'

You're Mr Bumble, Goinn thought; or a clone. Tall, stout, stupid, rich. Perhaps mum's idea's a good'un after all. I can make this thing my creature.

'I'm sorry, sir,' he said, all shy and humble. 'I'm a new boy here at Eton, and my mater's gone and got me lost.'

'Oh I say! Bad show, what? *Quo vadis*, as they used to say in ancient Greece!'

'Beg yours?'

'Oh how low!' said the vision. 'Beg mine do you, you little sprat! Well that can be arranged! They're such a pain though, the ladies, aren't they?'

'My mother works here, sir. She is a dame.'

The silk shirt seemed surprised. Hand went to tousled head. A series of burbles escaped the pampered lips.

'A dame? Oh no, oh well, oh soz, I mean—'

Mrs Goinn took over seamlessly. She shook her head, she smiled, she clipped Gregor smartly round his earhole.

'The foolish child,' she smirked. 'My Gregor, sir – my Grigori – he knows nothing yet of School I am afraid. With a little discipline and a firm hand, however, I have high hopes of him. The Beak I service is called Monsieur Robinet, he's head of Taps, and I guess the quarters we are seeking are in another corridor. Mister…?'

'Oh I say, gosh, yes, oh yes, I…I'm Mr Shippam – Paste-Shippam to go the whole hog. Horus Nicholae de Peperpott Paste-Shippam if you want the full unvarnished truth as my dear Pa would say. Bit of a mouthful, what, I sometimes wish I had a less distinguished lineage but…well, you know ancestry, a cruel master when all's said and done. Back beyond the Domesday Book we go. That's Doomsday with one O.'

Beyond the Stone Age. Gregor Goinn smiled inwardly. Ripe for the plucking. Whatever else, his mother was no fool.

'Not yet quite a Dame,' she said self-deprecatingly, 'but my trajectory is ever upwards, Mr Shippam-Paste.'

'Oh I say! It's Paste-Shippam, actually. But you can call me sir – it's so much less…so much more…'

Patronising, thought Grigori. Excellent. Give me the bullets, Horus, and I'll fire them. The pleasure will be mine.

'And my son may call you Horace, sir? The age gap is not so great.'

He actually blushed. He had never heard of anything so impertinent. This thing looked like a cockroach! Small, and bent, peculiarly ill-formed, not even in tie and tailcoat yet. Call him Horus? Wrong! Unheard of!

But faced with this woman who was barely half his size, he felt his courage fail. Oh gosh. Oh what? Oh jeepers! He must screw it to the sticking post, as the great Bard of Avon had said, quite possibly. He wrote in English, not in a noble ancient tongue, so it hardly mattered.

'My name is not Horace, actually, woman, but is Horus. It is a distinction of the utmost importance.'

My God, thought the cockroach. He's a coward too. His mother's smile was warm and crafty now.

'Aitch Oh Ar You Ess,' she enunciated. 'How very important, sir. How very noble. So my little Gregor shall call you Horus. How generous you are. We are humble folk, sir. Extremely humble.'

'And you can call me—' the son began.

'Anything I damn well please! Let's get this straight, you little insect! I'm your superior and I always will be! It is the way of School!'

Bravo, thought Grigori. That, you prat, is exactly what I have in mind.

'Bow to your master,' Dame Goinn told her bent and dark-faced child. 'Cream rises, as I've always told you, son. The best man is on top!'

'Now get out of my chamber, twisted boy. Ma'am, there's a room empty down the corridor, turn left, turn right, you'll know it by the smell. When you become a Dame in full reality I suggest it's in another house. Or else you will grow old licking this homunculid to shape! And now – dismiss! I need time to contemplate on higher things.'

First day, first meeting. All three of them went on their ways rejoicing. Except that Horus Paste-Shippam did not have to move.

Dulce decorum, as he chose to put it. Home sweet home.

Two

Alone once more in his invaded chambers, Horus Nicholae strutted around the bedroom in something of a bate. The snivelling little wretch, he thought. He'd sneaked in without a by your leave and stood there to be found as bold as brass.

His room, of course, his chambers, his alone. His florid face went white with anger as he recalled the little cockroach thing wearing out his carpet.

'As bold as brass!' he spluttered. 'As bold as bloody blithering! In my room, the unbearable little toad, my room, MY ROOM, MINE! What in the name of Hades was he doing in my room?'

And with his rather charming mater, too. Not all that ancient for a dame – a would-be dame – not half the age of his own dried up prune, and with a lovely pair of hooters, very suckable.

The moonface softened under its shock of unruly hair, and he ran a loving hand through it, his pride and joy, his set piece feature. It was soft and soothing to his touch, a unique colour, pale golden, with red and amber highlights. What Goinn's mother, he learned later, dubbed tart's hair, though that was the voice of jealousy, clearly.

Alone and stroking, he let the softness of his locks lull him into schoolboy thoughts. The mother's jugs were unobtainable, temporarily at least, but the strange angles of her son had a charm all of their own, and would soon live down the corridor. And need a guiding hand.

'Well,' he heard emerging from his rose-red lips, in his imagination, 'well Mr Cockroach – do you know how to play the girl?'

'Beg pardon, sir?'

The lips now twisted with delight. This beast was so wonderfully *low!*

'"Beg pardon?" What sort of school did YOU go to? You're a grammar schoolie, ain't you? How irrevocably LOW!'

The cockroach smiled. It was beyond erotic.

'Do you mean in bed, sir? I don't know, sir, for I've never tried. But I'm well aware I…'

'Owe me one? You do, young man, indeed you do. If you weren't so desperate ugly I'd bum you on the spot. Why *are* you so ugly, by the way?'

'I didn't even get to grammar school, I'm sorry sir. I went to a comprehensive. Flying Bull Lane.'

'A comprehensive? I think I've heard of one of them. Interesting name, though. Quaint.'

'We were called the Shitters, sir, the Flying Bull Shitters. And we hated grammar school boys as well. And girls.'

'Excellent. I have something in common with a common boy! What amazing trousers, by the way; like Oxford bags but something else. Did you say girls, though? You mean there are schools for the lower orders where the splitarse breed is also welcome?'

'Yes sir. More than welcome, sir. Well, within reason, obviously. It depends what use the split is put to.'

'Gross,' the big boy said. 'I've never sunk that low myself, I'm told they bleed and then have babies. I mean, how filthy, and it must play dreadful havoc with their muscles; do vaginas have a muscle anyway? And what if they bleed when the time is inappropriate? Oh double gross, then gross on gross on top of that. As my pater says, proof positive God's a woman and He don't like men at all. *Nole me tangerine, und so weiter*.'

'I'm sorry sir, I don't speak Latin. Flying Bull was not that sort of school.'

'That was Greek, *o ignoramus*. Now that *is* Latin. It means as thick as pigshit. *Nole me tangerine* is to do with oranges, as you might guess. Blood oranges.'

'The bleeding's not so bad in fact, sir, I believe that they have things for it these days. Sort of plug things they can pop up with a little blue string on, like a mouse's tail. A mouse's *bloody* tail, if you'll excuse the French.'

Ever capable of self-amusement, Horus Nicholae chortled, self love exhuding from his every pore. Exhuding? Was there such a word? He'd have to get his fag to google it. He googled it himself to show he had the expertise, and then called the new boy back next day, without his mater. This was exciting. This could go much further. This could lead to even better things.

'Gosh,' he said, on their second meeting. 'Gosh, for a grammar schoolie— Oh no, you said you wasn't, didn't you? But your talk of bIood and mouses' tails was quite hysterical in a minor way. But with your shitty education you don't even know what that word means, I imagine.'

'Hysteria's the stunt girls pull to get their way, I know that much, sir.'

'But what's it got to do with wombs, then? Hysteria and wombs, what's the connexion? I suppose you don't know that, do you?'

I know that you're an idiot, said Goinn to himself, and you've got money too, you reek of it. Oh God, how you love yourself.

'You don't, do you? Hence the vulgar silence. I feel you must apologise.'

'I'm very sorry sir,' said Gregor Goinn. 'Please forgive

me.'

A crafty look spread across the florid face.

'This girly thing,' the Big Blob said. 'Could you get me one? You know, in here, in my modest suite? Girls aren't allowed, the Head Beak says it lowers learning capabilities. But some of the bigger chaps…well. *Kudos*, is the magic word. Latin for always being at the head of the queue. *Ku*-doss.'

Goinn could see his chance. A plan was forming before his inner eye. Distasteful yes, but needs must when the devil drives. Mater had fucked him into Eton, and soon would fuck herself to damehood. Dame on the Game she called it, which was rather neat. She had enjoyed it, too.

'The trouble is,' he said, allowing his eyes to fill with tears, 'the trouble is, to use the rough slang of the comprehensive, I'm borassic lint.'

The stupid grin took on an eager air. Fat Boy was hooked.

'Borassic lint? Is that Greek or Sanskrit? *Sic* is Latin for unwell, and *borealis* is the northern lights, but what's lint got to do with it? I used to know a girl called Borealis once in fact, I paid her seven guineas to let me manualise her mammaries but she ran off with my cash. Which left me empty handed.'

'Bad.'

'Bad indeed, I had to pay another fifty for a chum

to beat her up for me. Cove with a sort of Latin name, in fact, which I can't reveal for fear of litigation. But he did a damn fine job, half killed her. I got sent a nipple as a token of regard. A job well done.'

'Manualise her mammaries?' Goinn mused. 'Oh, a feel of tit! Nice one, sir.'

'Nice two, in fact, but I like your turn of phrase, so wonderfully *earthy*. A feel of tit. I might use that. No attribution, naturally, it's copyright from now on, Ugly Youth, copyright to me.'

'And more than welcome, sir, it sounds much better from your lips. I'm flattered that you want to borrow it.'

'Borrow? I've been using it for *ages!* Ask anyone if you doubt my word, I—'

'Doubt you? Never! I heard it for the first time yesterday, straight from your lips.'

'Of course you did! Oh how we laughed And then you said *borassic lint*! Classic!'

'Which is rhyming slang, sir, which you taught me also. It means skint, you said, strapped for cash, down on one's uppers, broke. Sad truth though, is to persuade one of my ladies to do the deed with you, I'd have to pay her through the nose. And that comes expensive.'

'Well yes it would, cocaine's no longer cheap, is it? But do you mean prostitution, though? That's not allowed at Eton, *infra dig*. More Latin, I'm afraid.'

'Not prostitution, sir, never in this world. The money's just a way to help them improve themselves, get on by getting on, so to speak. I mean, sir, if you were of the poorer sort, and female to boot, wouldn't you jump at the chance?'

'Well, naturally. What chance?'

'To get up close and personal to one of the elite, sir. A chap like you, sir. If you could be persuaded to lower yourself so low.'

'On to a pauper's body? To penetrate a pleb's pudenda? Visit vulva vulgaris, both minor and marjoram, so to speak? A trip into another country, if you get my drift, with the emphasis on the initial syllable. That's cunt, in case you don't know a syllable from a syllabub.'

Or a silly bugger, Goinn thought. To his surprise he sort of liked this oaf, he liked his style, his unmitigated shite. Aimed carefully, such nonsense could be worth its weight in gold. To *him*.

Oh God, he told himself, I think I've found my meal ticket. Mum – you've dealt me the golden card. We've holed in one.

Three

Golfing aside, sex is Eton's other tradition of exceptionally long standing, as the art mistress said to the gardener. For many years it was purely boy on boy, largely because it's a religious school, and the Church believes that ladies' parts are irrevocably dirty, hence the posh name of *pudenda*: a thing of shame.

Gregor Goinn's mother, having seen them mincing to and from the school in Windsor in their three hundred year old *uniformius buffoonius*, had realised from an early age that they were tragically repressed, and almost certainly incapable of normal shagging duties.

This was a pain to her, because (again from an early age) she had liked what her own mother referred to as 'a bit of knob.' They were an earthy family, the O'Toolies, probably from Celtic roots, as Granny was extremely fond of stout and farting. So from eight years old (maybe nine and three quarters, but who's counting?) little Ejaculata was almost excessively fond of masturbation.

Before that, even, probably. She developed a special

relationship with her first gollywog (this was in less enlightened times, remember) and was heart-broken when Sambo was committed to the dustbin of *racio-descrimeo* history and replaced by a large white dolly with Aryan features, detachable limbs, and frilly knickers.

Underneath the knickers, by a quirk of plastic moulding, Katie Hopkins (as it was called) had a rather prominent *mons veneris*, which her owner discovered quite by accident one day afforded extraordinary sensation when rubbed against her own soft and needy parts. They were soon inseparable, and Ma O'Toolie could never work out why the knickers never needed washing, and indeed appeared to never have been worn.

The first time Katie and Ejaculata enjoyed climactic sex together, the human of the partnership discovered another thing about herself that some girls and ladies never do. Her orgasm produced a gush of fluid, and left a stain on the sofa she would have found difficult to explain had her mother been the slightest bit upset.

In fact, she had to bring the subject up herself, because Google was for once of little help, and her mother told her proudly that she'd joined a quite exclusive club who 'squirted just like men, without the need for grease or Vaseline.' Her name, though, should have been a giveaway, she added, as she'd 'actually been christened Immaculata, don'cha know? Now run and tell your grandma, she'll give you a chocolate egg.'

So Jackie, when she first saw the 'Eton Wankers' in the local streets, decided she might 'lend them a hand' if the opportunity arose. Or anything else arose, come to think of it. She had a fine imagination, did Ejaculata, and could well imagine that underneath those absurd trousers there might sleep an organ that would respond just like a good'un to something soft and moist.

A vagina, say, with the pre-orgasmic lubricant that leaked into her gusset at the thought of being nudged at; or failing that, a mouth. Eton boys, she guessed, would be repressed enough to want a bit of biting, a bit of scraping of the shiny purple bit with none-too gentle teeth. The *glans*, that was the word (Google this time; it could come good if pressed; like her).

But when would she get the chance, she wondered. They strolled in packs, did Eton boys, for fear of mockery, of even 'half a wall brick' in the words of the classic Punch cartoon. And she'd overheard them talking, and it sounded like the quacking of strangulated ducks, and their top hats and collars were crazier than their waistcoats. Improbability on legs. Surely no penis, or anything like that at all?

She must find out. She must, she must, she must.

Her thirteenth birthday arrived, and she was still a virgin. Fourteenth, but only just. She was getting the hang of it with some of the local boys, and she developed the technique of always coming long before they did (no mean trick for a convent girl). Which meant she could leave them hanging if they got too cheeky, and laugh at them if they tried to boast. She met one lad in Lidl of a Saturday, and when he told his friends he's 'shagged her rigid the night before' she said, extremely loudly, that he'd come into her hand before she'd got a proper grip of it.

'Not only that,' she added, 'but his hair was all over the place with excitement, and needed slicking down, so I used his come as hair cream. It made him look respectable but, ooh, that smell of Brobat!'

She was with her friends, as he was with his, but hers included Grandma, which destroyed the boys entirely with red hot shame. Not her, though, nor her granny. Both found it was delightful and Grandma, in fact, told them all what Brobat was, in case it had been before their time. When they were asked to leave by a store detective on grounds of bad behaviour, she told him to fuck off.

She was fourteen and three days when she got Brexit done – his name being Brian and his exit extremely rapid – and as she told her friends afterwards it didn't even touch the sides. Whip it in whip it out and wipe it was the formula in those days, which suited her exactly. She'd had her own fun, and much more through the act of torturing the prat. The whipped cream on the muffin (or on the grass, in fact) was making him come at the moment she ejected his penis with a monumental fart.

He actually cried, she told her best friend Jannie later, which wasn't true but made her feel even more contented with the 'grand deflowering.' It got better still nine months later when Jannie (a notorious copy-cat) produced her own first illegit.

'Independence never was your strong point, was it,' Ejaculata said. 'Have you actually got a brain?'

So Jannie got her own back by producing four more brats before her sixteenth birthday, because, she said, 'she just loved little bastards.' She was lying, naturally, and had them all adopted on the spot, except the black one, which nobody in Windsor would give house room to.

It taught Jackie another priceless life lesson, however. People could get round any amount of shame and misery by pretending that they liked it, and that they'd done it because they wanted to. Her own son (Cockroach as she called him) learned this at his mother's knee. It was one of the first and strongest parts of the philosophy that he passed on to his Eton chum.

Eton. That hothouse for all sorts of loony doctrines and perversions. If Gregor ever had a daughter he would call her Eugenica, he decided, and she would be as smart as he was. Another life lesson: think yourself intelligent (and fair, and honest, and trustworthy), and you will be in the eyes of the moronic masses. Who'd apparently been put on earth by God the Great Eugenicist to make his fortune.

Jackie, naturally, had learned her life lessons from her ma and grandma, the main one being spotting opportunities. Once she'd got the hang of manipulating other people's orgasms to further her enjoyment of life (and balls to sex; she'd never had a better come than the ones she shared with Katie Hopkins and her plastic pussy) she set about deciding what she wanted from the future, and how to go about it.

First of all she'd learn to read and write, then to research what made old England tick. By which she meant how was it ruled, who the rulers, who the scum. And whether wealth meant power (yes), did class still play a part in Britain (yes), and did race have any importance in these enlightened times. (Ho bloody ho.) As for Europe and America – well, even Barack wasn't really black, was he? Trump said he was an Arab Muslim who wasn't even born in the United State of A, and Trumpie wouldn't lie, would he? If you asked him if his father was a Klansman and his granddaddy a German Nazi you might get shot, but what the hell? He didn't like rude questions. They were rude, so rude, soooo rude.

So Ejaculata had to hatch a plan. She would have a baby, and she could take her pick from any man in Windsor to father it, except no blacks, no poor, no

Royalty. She never went to Burger King in Godalming, not even as a birthday treat, and she was her mother's daughter. Her mother's take on Royalty was this: they looked better hanging from a lamppost. She had French as well as Irish blood, maybe.

Like all good plans, her plan was simple. She read up exhaustively on Eton, discovered (surprise surprise) she couldn't go there, so worked out the quickest way to bypass that sexist rule.

Not for herself, *bien sur* (French blood, see? Confirmed). A sex change did not appeal at all; bad enough to bleed once monthly, far worse to squirt out Brobat each time someone copped a feel. Added to which, transgender was the new pariah state: just read the Daily Mail.

An Eton husband then? Bollocks. She knew and liked gay men, but she knew and hated teachers at her target place of learning. Learning? That was bollocks too, and double bollocks. They claimed to think Latin was important to a proper grasp of English, with Greek the icing *supra la cakeo*. Bollocks once more, and thrice times bollocks too (that's five, if you care to think about it. Possibly.) Latin taught you to show off your schooling, and Greek the difference between an ordinary beer in Athens and a *megalo*.

Mostly, Latin was useful for writing letters to the Daily Telegraph, which would be corrected by other pedants on the grounds of linguistic purity that could go on *diem per diem outa sightium.* The letters editor of the Telegraph, not many people know, is the highest paid wanker on the staff. Friends, this story is true; I used to be that woman.

Teachers, as Ejaculata found out instantaneously, were the weirdest of the whole weird Eton breed. They weren't even called 'teachers' but Beaks, and the Master meant the boss beak, even if she was a female, which she wasn't. Women were allowed on the staff, but only doing the things that women do best – be inferior. Each master had a dame, and while he did all the important stuff (teaching, shite like that) she looked after the 'welfare' of the boys. They weren't called pupils or students but Bobs, wet if they rowed boats and dry if they played cricket or football. Not any sort of football though, but Eton's special version. They couldn't play in local leagues. How neat is that?

There was another sport, however, as Jackie quickly learned, and it was called the Eton Wall Game. Along one side of one of the playing fields was a low brick wall, which prefects (Big Bobs) were allowed to sit on if they so desired. Non-prefects (Bobshites) were not, on pain of a kicking or a licking, depending on the predelictions of the punisher. Ejaculata tried hard to understand this game, but it's near impossible. You have to be a boy. You have to have blue blood. And be prepared to shed it for the honour of God knows who or what. A goal is scored every seven years.

Her final beau, chosen from the ranks of Beaks when she'd finally screwed her way upward through all positions (laundry girl, bed-changer, wang-wiper, wetdream-diviner), took her to a Wall Game to impress her. He seemed to think the sight of sweaty schoolboys pushing other sweaty schoolboys backwards and forwards along a line of bricks would have the knickers off her in a trice, and later on she proved that he was right. It would have been much easier and quicker if he'd just asked her in the first place, but there you are. Three seconds later she'd made him come, and didn't even bother for herself.

The Eton Wall Game is boring beyond all belief, and Ejaculata suffered badly for her kindness in agreeing to pretend to watch it. It contains no punching, bites or kicking, indeed no bugger all. The teams stood and pushed and grunted along the red brick wall, with the smell of sweat the only thing that kept her from nodding off. She liked a sweaty man, did Jacky. It reminded her of her Uncle Sid.

In his bed that night, she asked Rupert (she never got to know his actual name) what the Game was all about, and he launched into an exposition so staggeringly banal she had to *simulate* an orgasm because she couldn't wait the uncountably short time it normally took to get there by herself. It was a bloody good one, too, so apparently earth-shaking that she could reasonably pretend she'd gone to instant sleep afterwards, or even passed out with excitement; even died. And Rupert, so delighted at his wonderful technique, had a quiet wank to round it off. Amazing the skills a girl picked up at School.

But the deed was done, the fish was hooked, and God willing, it wouldn't be much longer before she could produce a son and heir. She was earning lots of money (in her low caste Windsor terms) already, and Rupe was so loaded she could not believe it when she hacked into his bank account. First off, she told him, she had a burning ambition to be a dame. Apart from him and his lovely body, it was her heart's desire. A little boy child would be the cherry on her cake. Cherry for my cherry, she lied furiously, and Rupert went pink with joy.

'The first?' he cooed. 'You mean I was the very very first? But that is wonderful! It's School, see, it's the Eton way! Superiority is embedded in our genes!'

What you just embedded in my jeans was very little to do with superiority, she thought – then burst into tears.

'What's wrong?' he cried. 'Oh darling, what is wrong!?'

'Nothing, you goose,' she sobbed and snuffled. 'It's…

it's…Oh darling, it is gratitude. Oh darling, darling Rupert, that you should have chosen me! And our little lad will go to Eton! Just think of it!'

She overwhelmed him with another flood of tears, and a quick orgasmic flood into the bargain. This love affair could be a lot of fun, she thought. Then thought of his bank balance, and another three more comes came roaring through.

Then she remembered her other little son, the one she had already, the little Russian-speaking cockroach called Greg or Grigori that she'd got more or less legitimately, from her awful husband Whatsisname. Lawful, sorry.

Well this one would be different. She'd cut her fags down to sixty five a day throughout the pregnancy, and only drink gin with lots of tonic, not neat like she preferred it. As a bonus she'd give up sex with Rupert (oh the loss, the loss!) unless he told her it was part of the bargain: her new baby would not get a freebie place at Eton if he didn't get his end away.

Ah well, not a problem when it came to it. There was always Mrs Hand and her lovely daughters to keep her happy and contented, and a couple of the dustmen who did the Eton bins were as discreet as they were wonderfully hung. She would get by.

The first time that he tried it, though, Ejaculata came on all hoity-toity.

'What do you think you're doing, Rupe,' she blurted, as he stuck his hand right up her skirt (not far enough luckily to make her come unscrewed, as the old joke has it). 'Do you think that I'm some sort of tart? Mistress Easy, as Shakespeare might have put it?'

'Quickly,' responded Rupe, ever the Beak even with his dick out. 'It was Mistress Quickly, Henry the Fifth, unless I'm much mistaken.'

'Well you are,' said Jackie. 'I'm neither easy nor quick. In fact what makes you so attractive is the fact you made me come at all. Most men—'

'Most men? But you're a virgin, aren't you? Most men what?'

'Oh take it as a compliment. Most men wouldn't have got within a yard of me. It's just that you— Oh Rupert, I do so love you so.'

'And you don't call anyone else Rupert, do you? It's a pet name? Just between the two of us?'

She simpered sweetly, through new-flowing tears. Christ, she thought, just between the two of us. Rupert – if you only knew!

Four

It took a bit of training, naturally, before the fruit was ready for the plucking. Although still very young (thirteen, if anybody's counting) Horus Nicholae had a wonderfully inflated sense of his own importance in the world.

His rooms in college, for instance. While every boy was entitled to a room, there were rooms and rooms, it was like in any other walk of life.

On his first day he had attended with his mum and dad (pater and mater, or *vice versa* once again) and an exclusive retinue of essential household staff, to be shown around by the Lord High head, or the Master, as he was called. In those days the Master was employed above all else for his nose.

His nose for money, that it. For cash, for moolah, or for pelf. Or, as the school would call it, *class.* One of the strangest, and most noticeable phenomena of the school had been, since not so long after King Henry had founded it for what he called poor boys, the amazing number of times that class and money went hand in hand. Poor boys could come, and more than welcome, but only if their dads were rich. Lo and behold, those that were were also steeped in *class*, they positively reeked of it. Some were extremely poor, as well; some were the sons of men as low as *baronets*, for pity's sake.

But they all had *class*. Strange, wasn't it? King Henry must have had a nose for that sort of thing himself. Maybe that's why the populace voted him in as king; true democracy. And when young Horus de Peperpott was presented by his ma and pa (democracy again, or demotics anyway), it wasn't the fact they'd brought their lad by helicopter, and he had lots of names, and lots and lots of servants, it was just something about him, something indefinable.

His father was a journalist, for Christ's sake. Leader writer on a magazine he just happened to be the owner of himself, the exclusivity of which was exceeded only by the exclusivity of its readership. Three hundred and seventy seven of them, in a good week, and all of them lords and ladies, even the mistresses.

The lower orders were allowed to peruse as well, as long as they could afford the cover price and hadn't been blackballed. It was a witticism much repeated in the board room that the reason no known reader was 'among our coloured brethren,' was that such types had been blackballed by Mother Nature. Only politicians were allowed outwith this rule, and only if they'd been to certain London clubs.

'What is his name?' the Master asked the father, and froze the mother with a look when she began to answer out of place. Her son, though, got there before her.

'My name is Horus Nichol—'

'And who was asking you, boy? We teach discipline at Eton, starting now. If you get a place here – which so far seems rather much in doubt – you will learn many rules. Of which number one is—'

There was a loud crack as Mrs Paste-Shippam reached across her son's head to smack a young household retainer behind him in the face. He did not flinch, he hardly even blinked; good jobs are hard to find since zero hours.

'Taken like a man,' the Head Beak told Horus. 'Now you may speak.'

'I didn't feel a thing,' said Horus proudly. 'I thank you for your trouble, sir.'

The Head Beak frowned.

'Do you find it acceptable that you should be stricken by a woman, though?'

'Not a woman, sir, but my mater. And that is different, sir.'

'I bore him,' said his mother. 'That makes me unique.'

Mm, thought the headmaster. Not exactly, madam, for you bore me too. He gave a charming little bow.

'A princess among mothers,' he said. 'Nay, veritably a quean.' With an *a*, he thought. A veritable quean. He turned back to the would-be scholar.

'Now child, do not keep me waiting any longer. I have a fine amontillado I wish to ply your mother withal. What was your name again, pray? Spit it out.'

'I'll do no such thing, sir. I've read a digest of the Fixtures, and rule Twenty Seven A, I do believe, is specific on that point. No gobbing in the quad.'

The Top Beak was beaming.

'Rule Twenty Seven B, in point of fact,' he said. 'A is anal eructation in ear or noseshot of the Royal Presence, whether Queen or Corgi. And we do not use low words like that in any case.'

'What should I say, sir? Surely not farting?'

'There is nothing wrong with that word, nor gobbing either, both are in the OED. The offending word, young man, is quad. School is a school with great traditions. Although many of our Old Boys go there – making up as much as seventy three per cent in some years – Oxford's use of quadrangle is *infra dig*. We'll be expecting better things of you.'

'Oh I say!' said Horus Nicholae, blushing like a milkmaid feeling her first teat, 'that means I'm in sir, does it? Oh I say!'

'Is your father loaded? Of course he is. The only thing I need to know now is your name. I expect to see it on the honours board before much longer. Your name, boy. *Full Moniker!'*

Now Horus was a happy boy (he had no reason not to be, did he?) and he loved above all else the sound of his own name. So mellifluous, so special, so *distingu*é (the Greek word for shit-hot). He drew a deep breath, and his chubby cheeks took on a glow of great self-satisfaction.

'My names are these, sir,' he enunciated. 'Horus Nicholae de Peperpott Paste-Shippam, erstwhile Shippam-Paste. I exhort you never to forget it, sir, for one day it will be on everybody's lips. My ambition, sir, is to be rich and famous and all-powerful. I promise you one day, sir, I will be the King.'

'Of England?' The headmaster put on a face. He'd met this sort of boy before, crammed full of shit in any language. 'Well, sir, king of England is a fine ambition.'

'*Cojones,*' young Nicholae replied. 'Which is the Greek for testicles, as I'm sure you know.'

'You speak Greek already do you, boy? Impressive.'

'And Latin too. And Welsh and Dutch both plain and double. But *cojones* will do in this case, sir. I will be King not just of England – although England is the very very best, the *nadir* as men say – but of the World.'

'Top of the world?' the head man smiled. He put on his Cagney accent. 'Top of the world, ma?' And when he saw the reference had missed its mark, 'Oh never mind.'

'I said King, not top, but Top will do if you're lacking in ambition. King of the World, sir, that is me. Just watch this space.'

The Big Beak nodded affably, smiling at dear pater.

'Very good,' he said. 'He's only the third future king to be enrolled this term, and they are kings already.'

'Not of the world, though,' Horus spluttered. 'There are king and kings, sir. There are, there are, there are—'

The Head Beak made a gesture to his father. Power finding money.

'If you step into the office, sir, my staff will put him in the register,' he said smoothly. 'Cash or card; anything will do. No contact free however, the sums are far too great. No credit, either. Eton did not get where it is today by giving credit.'

'Hallelujah,' brayed Horus Nicholae de Peperpott. 'Credit is for scum, not future Kings. And especially not Kings of the World.'

Five

By the time Gregor Goinn set his eyes on Horus, his chosen mentor was ensconced in the best set of chambers in the best building of the ancient school. He had the best chambers, in the best house (Excremont), and was the best masturbater of the full twelve hundred boys.

This was a boast he made himself, and nobody ever challenged it. He could pull his pud at least four hundred ways, all of them guaranteed to give total satisfaction, accompanied by painful swelling and perhaps a little soreness. But *nihil wanko sufferandum* (Greek) was his watchword, and he took his fellow students' laughter for an expression of their natural jealousy.

The sad truth was, however, until he met the boy whose mother had wormed her lowlife son into the school by her wiles at willy-waggling, that this was his only useful boast. The Eton system of education was designed not to educate, but to groom the mediocre to reach the top. Some pupils, though, were so ridiculously dim they could hardly hope to make the bottom rung. De Peperpott, his fellows speculated with delight, might be one of them.

Masturbation, for example. Most of the boys were more than adequate, but many of them saw it as a step to higher things. Striving to achieve, in any language, was the base motto of the school, and achievement, in most boys' eyes, was leaving the pud within the underpants when possible, to get it stuck into something more enticing than a grubby hand.

There are females at Eton, obviously (after all eight hundred staff are needed to pamper the young rich). For a start the Dames are girls (though that is deemed a demeaning epithet, though sadly necessary), as are the cleaners and the laundry maids. Others, too; any task beneath a male who breathes the sacred air of School is relegated to the ladies. And many of these girls, of course, are masturbators in their own right, although not prone to boasting of it as are the boys. And others yet, a sizeable minority, are not adverse to a little bit of dick.

Horus Nicholae had heard of this, not once but many times. In fact, whenever he was allowed to be in the company of his 'friends' for any length of time outside of eating and straining in the communal doorless lavatories – a school tradition deemed to be a fine way to harden up a boy – it was the main topic of conversation. He quickly learned that tales of high-jinks in the privacy of his own pyjama bottoms were considered less than fascinating, and even communal gropings of the weaker new bugs (rectum ragging) weren't considered up to much in terms of high achievement.

It took him some good while to realise that the 'pokings and the porkings' that his fellow students bragged about involved not the pretty little buttocks of third-formers, but actual females. The ones he saw in mob-caps and aprons, with brushes and dusters in their rough-chapped hands. The ones down in the sickbay who smelled of disinfectant. It occurred all in a rush one afternoon, when a Drybob lost his teeth during the Wall Game, and the nurse who leant over him was goosed by fourteen boys before his very eyes.

He was good at the Wall Game, was wee Nicholae. For he was not so wee, in fact, but had grown up big and beefy, because he ate so much and wanked the calories away. At the Wall, also, the others could not avoid him however much they wanted to, which was (apparently) the point of it. You never saw the ball, you hardly moved an inch, you just grabbed a hunk of nearby flesh and pushed and shoved and ground and gouged until the scrummage came to a final halt and you all went home to tea. Maybe you'd won, maybe you'd lost. Nobody seemed to know or care.

Just because he was good at the Wall game did not

mean he became attractive to the girls, however. It was his stupid face, really, and his tendency to puppy fat, and a haircut like a startled cherub. Some of the dames might have enjoyed taking his clothes off, given half a chance, but as he discovered later, as an adult, it was because women tend to seek the childish in a man, and love to mother them, even to the extent of bringing long dead mammaries back into service for a suck.

There was another pathway to success at Eton. Although the school was crap at games in most respects (they even have their own versions of rugby and football to hide the fact they can't win by playing to the normal rules), when they detected the tiniest potential in a boy, they went ape-shit for him. Often helped by the fact that parents, realising how thick their offspring were, poured money into the team games like there was no tomorrow.

Hence, in years to come, the Peperpott Pavilion, and the Nigel Farridge Garridge, where the Beaks all keep their cars, as long as they aren't made in Europe. The top hat shop, similarly, is sponsored by one of the dimmest of the old boys, who was painted by Sir Joshua Renolds-Chayn reclining on the front bench of the House of Commons with his nanny, Alma Mater.

In the Peperpott Pavilion, to this day, visitors can still see, (on payment of a small fee), the blue plaque commemorating Horus's finest achievement at the crease.

This sporting prowess, then, did guarantee he would get something useful from his time at school. His failures in other subjects were grim even by Eton standards, although it did not mean he could not boast about them. Sums? You must be joking. Geography? After five whole years he still did not know the difference between Austria and Australasia (where?). History? Boring and inaccurate: did you know England no longer had an Empire? Bollocks! Art? Bummer Stoke-Bramlingshurst, head of that department, only ever wanted to daub him naked with poster paint and melted chocolate.

The only good thing that happened was when a man called Fogarty introduced him to the so-called classic languages. Strangely for a school that provided half the Foreign Secretaries and two thirds of British Ambassadors in every government for about two hundred years, scarcely any of them spoke any of the languages beyond the rankly shite. And Mr Fogarty, in despair at last, went and opened up a pub in Pwllheli and thereafter spoke only Welsh.

But when he realised this dumbcluck would never get the lowest pass grade in Greek or Latin, Mr F compiled for him an extensive cribsheet of the most essential phrases for showing off, and made him learn them all by heart.

'Just drop them into conversation randomly, and

if anybody challenges you, cite original manuscripts which you alone had access to in libraries like the Louvre, the Uffizi, and Oldham Mumps. If they go on being difficult, say how much you pity them, and ask them if they've ever heard of Josef Fogarty, Bard of Bards at East Cheam Eisteddfod, 1941. Then threaten them with a defamation action. Works like a charm.'

Despite his lack of any talent, young Horus (or *Peperpllt Og* as Fogarty called him in Irish/Welsh) put this into practice, tentatively at first but with increasing confidence. On another hint of Mr Fogarty he joined the press, having obtained a dismal pass degree at Oxbridge despite expending thirty seven thousand pounds in bribes and twenty more for sight of final papers before the exams, and learned the instant benefit of an Eton education. Within minutes of his father announcing his son's interest in the third estate, he had offers from all the top papers in the land.

The Telegraph? Of course. The Times? Well, need you ask? The Mail damn nearly took his arm off but his mother didn't like their knitting patterns, and Mr Murdoch, of the Sun, pointed out that own his expensive education (in the best school in Australia) was a carbon copy of everything they taught at Eton, but with a slightly less ridiculous accent. The Express tried hard, the Mirror (for a joke?). and then the mighty weeklies, with the Spectator in the lead, and the National Front

Bugle snapping at its heels.

'By Jove!' said the winning editor. 'This chappie speaks Greek just like a native! That's what I call class!'

That word again. Because of it, and to ease him into this hard-working life, they proposed a hundred thousand, for ten articles a year.

'That's not enough.' said Peperpott. 'I—'

'Oh all right then, two hundred.'

He'd meant not enough articles, just ten a year might be rather boring. He wanted more trips; more lunches; more expenses; more adoring ladies to impress.

'But that really might be our last offer,' said the editor. 'We're already having to sack eleven proper journalists to pay you that. We could say guineas, I suppose.'

'Quite right, too. I went to Eton, after all. I was president of Pop. If you want quality, you've got to pay top whack. Anyway, proper journalists are scum.'

The deal was done. On a handshake, as was the Eton way. It would save both parties tax.

They went and drank champagne.

Six

Journalism is easy, you ask anyone. Horus Nicholae de Peperpott Paste-Shippam had asked his new amanuensis (Greek) on the first day that they met, after they'd got through his dreams of dirty girls, and blue-tailed tampax.

'I say, cockroach,' said the Eton wag – 'you don't mind if I call you cockroach, do you, it suits your demeanour. Should I be a scribe, dost reckon? On one of the noble right-wing rags?'

'If you have no interest in the truth, sir.'

'I've never told a lie, young Grigori. Never ever ever in my life.'

'So an interest in the truth is irrelevant. You need not bother with it. You're a philosopher. Quite brilliant.'

Nicholae de Peperpott laughed so hard he nearly soiled his pants. He hugged his sides and spluttered as he laughed.

'That is so *killing!* Oh humble cockroach, that is such a *hoot!* I'll speak to ma and pater forthwith. I shall become a famous scribe. Eton and Oxford! The classic path to glory!'

'And all on talent. Every last morsel and iota down to you. I'll be so proud to be your fellow traveller.'

You're stupid, thought the humble cockroach, and his plan was almost fully formed. He saw a future in the sunlit uplands. This fat, conceited boy would be his meal ticket. And then his fortune.

He also noticed that the bigger boy had made himself strangely excited. He was panting, his eyes were hot and droopy, and he was gazing at the hated cockroach in a most unhating way. Good lord, thought Gregor Goinn, the fruit is ripe for plucking, I must brace myself again. The sex will be extremely transient, but the aftermath could guide my life for ever. And my bank balance.

'Journalism is very good for starting out,' he said, 'but for you, sir, there are surely higher things. With me behind you, we might forge a formidable machine. I'm thinking politics, plus the path to power in this great democracy is often through the law. Do you fancy taking silk?'

'Silk?' panted de Peperpott. 'Silk, rayon, cotton, just so long as you will tear it off me! I want a woman, creature, and you promised you would show me how!'

'Indeed I will, sir, and I mentioned money, also. But that was before I truly knew you. I know now you are above such things and so am I! Now bed, Horus, oh please, the bed, the bed!'

The belt and buttons of his britches were unloosed already, and the cockroach, all limbs and angles and a little poky thing, was flying through the air to where his masterful seducer, blonde, tousled and sweaty, had thrown himself onto the bed like something from the grand old opera.

The congress did not last for long – less than a half a minute – and neither boy enjoyed it much, as the cockroach cock was hardly big enough to inflict real pain.

No money changed hands either, but Goinn got something of far more worth than cash from the encounter. He convinced his partner in the sweetest, saddest terms, that to lose your virginity to a person of the same sex meant that you were doomed to live a life of irrevocable shame. No one must ever, *ever*, know or Horus would be blackmailed to within an inch of his father's gigantic bank balance.

'It is our secret, dear Nicholae,' he murmured through his tearful simpering. 'I promise you I will never, ever tell, for if it should come out, your future life will be a ruin. Be schtum, forever schtum, and trust in me. Trust me, my little Peperpott, and no one else. Nobody.'

Had Nicholae been a little brighter, it might have occurred to him that half the other buggers in the school were buggering each other morning noon and night, high days and holidays included. Even the Muslim pupils, apparently, as long as they said three Hail Marys afterwards. And no one cared. No one in the whole wide world.

'And if your mother ever knew,' said Gregor, with finality, 'it would kill her. It is our secret, my dear, dear friend, and it will go with us unto the grave.'

When Horus fancied another little go a half an hour later, the cockroach said he could not, for it was his time of month. One of the females in the latrine squad had a certain sort of pill, however, which if he could get one would make it possible just one more time.

'Oh Gregor, can you get one for us, please?'

'But sadly they are very dear, and as you know, I'm—'

'*Splint*.' It was enunciated with proud rotundity. 'That's Latin, you know. No, I suppose you don't, do you?'

'I said expensive,' said the cockroach, 'but I'm afraid extortionate would be a better word. A hundred guineas. Just for one.'

'A bagatelle!' laughed de Peperpott. 'Which is Greek for *no problemo*. But are you sure it's safe? It won't make you sick or anything?'

'Of course not, but then I don't take it, do I, it's for you. The man of the partnership. The one who does the work and gives the pleasure. Oh come on, dear friend, if you're really serious. Two hundred for cash. I'll catch her if I hurry, before she gets the bus to town. That's a hundred for the pill and another ton to buy her silence.'

'Ton? Is that the same as *tonne*? All my weights are *avoirdupois*, naturally. That's French for have some peas.'

'If we're talking French it's slightly dearer, sir. Two hundred and fifty five. The exchange rate. But do I need to call you sir now? Now that we're so very very *intimate?*'

'Of course you do, you oaf. Just because you've—'

He did not like to say the word. Suddenly it sounded vulgar. Fucking was what you did to girls. It was an anagram for receptacle, give or take.

'No, you must call me sir, it's fitting,' he continued, 'but I will call you Goinn, not Gregor. Christian names are vulgar, aren't they? Among friends.'

Goinn left the room in great contentment. So they were friends, were they? Well *excellent*, as Mr Burns might say. The deed was done, the deal was made. Dr Frankenstein had got his creature.

Seven

President of Pop was his first ambition. De Peperpott's, that is, not little Gregor Goinn's. He, as they lay back after their second congress of the first great afternoon (achieved again with no pain for him and no sensation either, except a fuller wallet) professed to not even know the phrase, and pretended to assume it must be somebody's dear father.

Horus laughed heartily at this. He did so relish ignorance in others.

'Pop, you hopeless little insect, not Pa! Not pa, not pater, not the dear old *moneybagus domesticus*. That's cod Greek, Goinn, not the real thing; if you get it wrong people will laugh at you, so listen carefully and learn.'

'Thank you, Nic—'

'*Sir* you blob. I'm not charging you for this knowledge, though. We must stick together now, like spunk to a blanket, eh? Don't worry by the way, about that. The maids are more than used to cleaning it away. I'm very prolific in that department, I'll have you know. You might say I'm a world beater.'

'As in everything you—'

'Put my hand to! I say, how droll, do you get it, Greg?'

'Indeed I do, Nic. I call you that because you called me Greg, sir. When rules are rules, it is as well to stick to them.'

'*Touché!* But rules, to me, are there to be broken. I am the King, and therefore make them up, the whole *shebang*. That's Hindi, by the way, a language spoken by our fuzzywuzzy friends, also known as Sanscrit. I hate to boast, but I am better at languages than any man I know.'

'World beater, sir, which is worth repeating. If things go badly, in whatever circumstance, you should say your reaction is world beating. A sort of bottom line.'

'You're teaching me to suck old eggs, my little cockroach. World class! World beater! I've always been world class, I'm famous for it!'

'But rules can sometimes be important. Rules can—'

'Balderdash and poppycock! You know nothing, scum, and less than less than nothing! I sometimes wonder how you ever got into School. Your father was in trade, I shouldn't wonder, which is the biggest insult any man can offer, so suck it down and choke on it. Did he run a Paki shop, perhaps? Maybe he's a market trader!'

He is, young Goinn acknowledged (to himself). He trades in certainties. Diamonds, platinum and gold, and stripping forests from the Amazon to Indonesia. So rich he wouldn't fund his son to go to public school, because incentive is the only way to give a boy a chance in life. And kicked his wife out on the same altruistic grounds, which is why she's now a dame and her cockroach is training up this self-indulgent twat to be top man.

Or President of Pop, at least. Lying on the rumpled bed, breathing in the smell of Brobat, Goinn learned of the fat boy's one Eton ambition, and decided that his own best step up the ladder would be to make sure he achieved it. First membership of Pop, then President. If Trump could make it in America, why in hell's name not? In light of that disaster, *anything* was possible.

Pop, for those of you who've never heard of Google, is the (so-called) secret society run exclusively by and for the richest human beans in the Windsor school. It's not dissimilar from the Castle just across the fields, or indeed the eponymous pub around the corner where Mail readers sometimes go in the hope of copping a look at something Royal. You get in Pop by invitation, and if one member doesn't like you, you get black balled and Bob's your uncle.

It's only got twenty members or so most of the time, and most of them, in theory, are good at sport. The real sport though is keeping others out, to maintain its unshakeable superiority. Its HQ is a scruffy room, with a scruffy open grate, and a scruffy little slattern called Sadie M'Gumdrop who rubs up the fire-irons when they get dirty, as she does indeed the boys too tired for a wank.

The best thing about it for young Horus Nicholae was the uniform. Not a uniform precisely – how low would that be to a classy bug – but the waistcoat only a Man of Pop was entitled to. Every boy at Eton wore a waistcoat, naturally, but these were something else.

Flamboyant to the nth degree, floral, scarlet, sky-bluepink, or any combination that you cared to name. Happy was the boy whose mother's servants could sew and do embroidery – one Popster's was the scrotum of an elephant, with precious stones lodged in the natural creases. Another's was bright scarlet red, with hairy thongs that peeped out through the button holes.

A normal boy, seen walking down Windsor High Street dressed like that and pissed, would have attracted the attention of the men in blue. But most Home Secretaries are Eton educated, so most arrests involve only black or Asian passers-by. All very friendly, though; they get nothing but a hearty slap, a fine, and a warning to 'never pass this way again.'

Perhaps the ostentatious dress code is the key. No Poppers are arrested, and none who are, indeed, are members of the club. Neat.

The first time Horus Paste-Shippam applied, he was devastated to be blackballed. Goinn, who worked on long-term plans to wreak his havoc, had insisted he would be welcomed, on the grounds of money.

'Rubbish,' Horus had brayed, 'Eton is not crass. It will be class that gets me in, that special something that can't be bought. You wouldn't understand, for you have neither. And when I'm in, I may not even talk to you, so there.'

On returning to his rooms after rejection – and Grigori was carefully not there – he was so upset he almost had a secret little weep.

He was an idle boy, however, with limited imagination beyond his dreams of kingship, so could think of no other way into Pop save bribery and crawling. He approached every chap he saw in a special waistcoat, and simpered, and swaggered, and sometimes dropped his wallet ostentatiously, packed beforehand with great care so that folded notes would fall out in profusion. This was in the days before banknotes were made of plastic, which nobody in Pop would pick up anyway, because they were so low. Plastics were good for snorting, but most Poppers thought cocaine a ladies' drug, so preferred heroin, or heroin mixed with weed, which they wittily called horseshit.

The Popsters knew him, naturally. This needy little fat-twat with the golden curly hair, bouncing along the road or corridor or by the Wall, expecting to be remarked on for his porky prowess at the famous game. The one who – if he ever got close enough to speak – would gush and guzzle about all the sports he loved, and how he'd heard the Pop room needed a new fireplace which he would love to replace with an antique one from an attic at his home and how it would be a pleasure and a privilege once he had got his membership.

He bought a little gold-covered notebook so that he could note down anything they said that might be worth recording for posterity, but the most printable was fuck off and die you hopeless twat. He wrote it down in any case. One day he'd render it into Ancient Greek or Latin. Class.

Had Paste-Shippam been more sensitive, he probably could have got quite upset by some of this boyish banter. But he was a rational soul, and knew damn well they could not really hate him, because he was, in short, so wonderful. It was a School thing, a tradition, a running of the gauntlet to sort out men from boys. He was certain – he was absolutely sure – that one day he'd be taken to one side and toasted in champagne, and begged to come on board, and to forgive them if they'd been a little rough or boisterous.

And then one day, he knew that it had happened. In the bathhouse, after a long and boring Wall Game, which his side had lost or won.

Stark naked in the steamy room, rigid with boredom and discontent because no one had said a single word to him since yesterday, he noticed a cohort of the bigger boys – bigger than him, much bigger – walking towards him in a naked phalanx. They were smiling, each and every face was wreathed in smiles, and each one had a towel in his hand, a wet towel, twisted like a rope.

'I say, chaps,' said Horus, pink with pleasure. 'The time has come, not so? *Tempus fugit*, and all that tosh! You've come to give me what I have deserved so richly, for so long!'

If that confused them, the confusion didn't last. With an upward flick between his chubby thighs to squash his tender ballbag, they knocked him down and fell upon him.

'Up school, up school, up school!' he heard them chanting, and then his ears were boxed till he was deaf. He came round later, still bollock naked. The room was empty, except for a cleaning lass who tutted at his blubbering then ignored him.

They'd beat him to a pulp.

Eight

Next morning, when the cockroach came to see him, he was still crying, still in bed, but still prepared to see the best of it.

'Cripes, sir!' his mentor said. He liked to drop into public schoolery, culled mainly from the Beano, to keep up the pretence. 'I say, have you had a leathering, or what? Name the cad, sir, and I'll give him what for!'

'What for? What rot!' said Horus. 'I say, did you hear that, I've made a *jew de mott.* It's an anagram, the same whichever way round it goes. Or do I mean a palimpsest? R O T, rot, T O R, ro— Oh buggery, you've made me get that wrong. And anyway, what do you mean by cad? There were at least eleven of them. It was after…'

'Ah, a Wall Game injury. But at least your team won or lost, I imagine, which is one thing. Shall I call a nurse, sir? Or is it bad enough to bother Matron?'

That dreaded word pulled de Peperpott up all standing. The matron was a thing of infamy, fierce, lathered in fake tan, and not a Priti sight. She was also a legend of stupidity, almost guaranteed to kill or cure, minus the second option.

'It was after the Wall,' Horus agreed, his voice stronger by the moment. 'I was set upon by all the louts at once, they might as well have been the working classes, they kicked me when I was down. One of them, at least, stamped on my scrotum. Look.'

'Painful. What had you done to deserve it?'

'I mentioned Pop. I may have offered them my services. But there are hidden rules apparently, procedures. A bit like the Masons, I believe.'

'Perhaps you had the wrong trouser leg rolled up, sir. But I take it now they've beaten you, they've asked you in?'

Two tears crept from the puffy eyes and down the soft unhealthy cheeks. The roses were intermixed with bruises now, a rather fetching blue.

'And I offered them my uncle's antique fireplace as well! He'd've killed me if he'd ever known, it's worth a fortune. At least a half a mill, I shouldn't wonder.'

'You didn't say that though, did you? I'm surprised you got out with your life. Do you want me in your bed to kiss it better? Where does it pain, exactly? Slip your trousers down.'

'Can't,' said Nicholae. 'Twould hurt too much. Too tender. In any case, I think this needs a woman's touch.'

Inwardly, the cockroach smiled. He'd done it as a

test, and the spoiled brat had passed with flying colours.

'We had a deal,' de Peper whined on. 'I want a girl, a woman, a receptacle for my shining fluid. Up the chuff-piece.'

'Boys can be a bore, can't they?' Gregor's voice was warm with sympathy. 'I shall miss your splendid organ, though, indeed I'll be bereft. But…'

But I'll always have it with me in the bank, he told himself. Blackmail's not a word I like to use, but it is extremely useful. Work on the shame now, Gregor, make him think there's nothing in the world more vile than boy on boy. Backside rules the Navy, so they say, but any half decent public schoolboy knows the second verse. Horus Salmon-Paste – I've got you by the short and curlies!

'So tell me what you really want, sir,' he went on 'What you really really really want, to quote those scrawny girls whose dirge has just gone to the top. What's more important, a bit of minge or you as President of Pop?'

There was no contest, obviously. Orgasm was transitory, and not urgent at the best of times. For Nicholae, now, it was the worst of times. He wanted to be President and they would not even let him cross the threshold.

'But can you swing it?' he asked, through broken

lips.

'Your organ, or a waistcoat and top hat? Yes, I can get you into Pop, but it will cost you, I'm afraid.'

'Don't be vulgar, beast; how much? When? Shall I send to mater for my best dress shirt and floppy tie, the azure one with scarlet wings? How much?'

'It's not the money,' Goinn lied, 'it's the learning that you've got to do. I must be frank, my friend, there is much you need to swallow.'

'I'll swallow anything. Alma told me it's what you have to do. You know Alma? Grease-Blobb's live-in nanny. He wears tails in bed with knitted woolly topper; his dress pyjamas. But what else d'you think I need to know?'

'Politics? Philosophy? Economics? Do you want to be in government?'

'No! Never in this world!'

'That's a good start. What do you want to be then?'

'Rich, powerful, irresistible to women, famed for my charisma; nothing much. Certainly nothing beyond my capabilities. My mama says—'

'Fuck mama,' said Gregor, brutally. 'Mamas are useless. They love their sons, and love is stupid.'

'I've got no worries there then, have I? She told me once she'd rather have had a female, and she didn't say a girl, she said a bitch. Have you never heard of Clytemnestra?'

Goinn had. He raised his eyebrows; inwardly.

'Mm,' he said. 'The thing is though, if you're not a politician in this country, you need another arrow to your bow. The qualities you aspire to are all quite well and good, but—'

'Well and good? They're excellent!. My qualities are—'

'World beating, yes. But remember, Horus, that is just a phrase. Without back-up, it's not worth a Filipino's fart.'

'And now you're being racist, Goinn! I'm beginning to regret I saved you from oblivion. I'm beginning to think that you're a waste of time.'

The cockroach liked that. To play the race card in complete defiance of the truth! This puling blob of privilege might have potential after all.

'Excellent, sir, you *can* fight back! I'll get you into Pop, I promise you, and as a bonus, into bed with girls as well. Have you seen the dhobiess that does the dirty dhotis in the dorm? The tall one, with eyes like gleaming diamonds and tits to die for?'

'Sizzling spaffballs, yes!'

'The princes of the Punjab have a special name for her. Tennisballwallahheadwallahboy. They positively drool.'

'They call her boy? Are they perverted? Most Indians are, you know.'

'Tut tut, who's being racist now? They call her that because her head is round and lovely, and her breasts are like twin Slazengers. Just thinking of them beats transcendental meditation.'

Nicholae clutched his crotch so hard his scrotum squeaked. Ouch. That blasted Wall Game.

'And I can fuck her, can I? And she's not in fact a chap? And will she…oh! Oh glory hallelujah, she is so very *brown*.'

'Now *concentrate*, before you pull it off, sir. We're talking Pop. We're talking President of Pop. Where girls will fall like rotting medlars in your path. All sorts of girls. White, black, pink, brown, bloody skewbald if you so desire. Girls are girls, sir, they are two a penny. They are of no importance in the world.'

'Skewbald and *lickerish*,' said Horus, dreamily. 'That's sexually excited, you know, which Welshmen do in lavvies with domestic hens. The lickerish bog black chickens, as Bob Dylan-Thomas wrote, the pervert. Fowl play! I say, another *jew de mott!* How neat is that?'

'Neat indeed, sir, but to get to be Top Pop you need a lot of other things. I can train you up with pleasure, but as you know, my rates are rather steep. That's a joke, sir. Everything, to *you*, is free.'

And that's a lie, he told himself. I'll take your cash off you, but also your self-respect, your name, your soul. First let me amuse myself by seeing how dedicated you are to the concept of the truth.

'It will also be a lot of work,' he said, 'so I must be absolutely confident of this. You're not a lazy sort of chap, are you?'

'Good heavens no!' said Horus Nicholae. 'You'll never meet a harder working bug than me, I'm like a dynamo!'

'And integrity? How are you on that? Or might I say on that *rare quality*?'

'The quality of mercy is not strained, and never will be Greg m'boy. That's a quote from Virgil, by the way, I know him off by heart, the leading Roman thinker of his time, high priestess of Macedonia after the tragic sex change. Not many people know that.'

'I didn't, sir, I must admit it. But I believe you're fluent in many ancient languages?'

'Eleven at the last count. The classics tutor at my prep school threw himself into the Hellespont in despair at keeping up with me in conjugating verbs. *Cocinco, cocincis, cocincit, concincimus, cocincitus, cocincunt*. That brought the house down at the international finals in Istanbul. I never got the gold cup, though. Never trust a Greek, eh!'

Gregor Goinn found all this wonderful. The chubby little liar, lying on his grubby little bed, swollen with pride at his supposed achievements, and his sore and tortured little scrotesack swollen also. Probably the richest boy who'd ever been turned down by Pop, a society whose standards were the lowest of the low.

We're going to go far, he told himself. This blustering mediocrity will be my shield against all comers. As he goes up I'll go up with him, and when he comes down I'll…I'll disappear.

Aloud, he said:

'I recommend a little olive oil for your noble *pudi*, sir, for when Tennisballwallahheadwallahboy gives it fifteen-love. *Pudi's* the Punjabi word for knob-end, so you'll need to get yourself some lubrication and some proper sleep. Is that correct Punjabi, *pudi*? Can you help me out?'

But strangely, the proper sleep had begun already. Leastways, de Peperpott was snoring gently, his tiny organ tender as a half-chewed prune.

He could not be feigning, could he? No. This boy never lied. He was a credit to his school, his house, and most of all to Good Old Ingerland.

And good old mum, young Gregor Goinn thought. There is truly nothing like a dame…

Nine

Money was the key to getting into Pop, of course it was, but where it was directed and by whom was what Horus Nicholae had no idea at all of, and no way of finding out. When he could walk again without limping he tried approaching other Wallgamers, half expecting Gregor's magic would have already worked, but quickly learned he was mistaken.

Jerkoffe Grease-Blobbe, who appeared to be the fount and arbiter of all unwritten Eton rules, allowed him to approach, sniggering behind his hand at his crippled gait.

'I say,' he brayed, 'have you ruptured something? The Wall Game's not for girlie-lads, you know, would you like some ointment to rub on it? Forty pounds a fluid ounce today. Nanny, have you got some in your hand-valise?'

Nanny, strangely, was quite a pleasant girl, and even more strangely was always with Grease-Blobbe, even in his private bathroom. As master of the Pop Police, however, he was able to stifle rumours, even when she turned up rather moist and dripping. He was a fervent Anabaptist (Yossarian Division), and capable, it was said, of making loose-tongued people disappear.

'Now, sir,' she told Jerkoffe quite severely, 'this young bug's done nothing to deserve such scorn. He's actually loaded and he wants to be in Pop.'

Grease-Blobb, like all Eton men (as they liked to see themselves) knew that money was the root of everything, and nanny was telling him this chap might be the way to his salvation. For nanny knew what few other people were yet aware of – her employer was in meltdown. His family, who claimed roots in the aristocracy going back to Domesday and beyond, were in fact a gang of chancers, who'd made their cash as wartime profiteers. Not the Norman Conquest war, not even the Napoleonic, but the First and Second and beyond. They stole scrap metal out of Scapa Flow, and out-wheelerdealt the hardest sons of Sarajevo. More recently they'd backed wrong horses, big time, and bet that Trump and Putin would play straight with them.

A few honours had come the Grease-Blobb way over time, indeed a shedload, but they'd cost a shedload also. So now he needed multo cash injections as his multo hedge funds all went multo bang, one behind the rest. Alma Mater had his back as usual though, it seemed. And for a humble nanny, Alma was financially shit-hot.

It was not Gregor himself who'd tapped into this lead it was his mother, through her tame beak Rupert. Like his famous namesake her Rupe was Australian, and he also had a weakness for much younger women. Ejaculata was only thirty four (give or take) but claimed sixteen and could have passed for less. A paedophile's delight.

After a long and complex talk-in with her son one day, she knew it was her duty to come up with something special to ease Horus's passage, so to speak. She staged a most orgasmic marathon, and when Rupe had had a shower and recovered, she hit him with the nitty-gritty.

'He wants to get in Pop,' she said.

'Who?'

'Don't play smart, Rupert, it doesn't suit you. My little boy.'

'Your little boy? You mean that fucking cockroach?'

He had to have another shower after that, for different reasons. While he was gone, Ejaculata had two or three more comes to clear her head. Time to dissemble.

'Look,' said Rupert, when they'd snuggled down again. 'I got wee Gregor in the school, all well and good, but Pop's much harder. Eton boys are meant to fight their own battles, aren't they? They're meant to get on in the world through brilliance and hard work.'

'What, like Anthony Eden, who lost us Suez? Bob Boothby, the Kray twins' chum? Jeremy Thorp, the well-known dog lover? Nigel Farage? Come off it, Rupe.'

He tried to lighten it.

'Well, there was Michael Bentine, he was in the Goon Show. And Lord Ormsby-Gore. His wife was also most extremely droll.'

'Eh?'

'My dear Mrs Ormsby-Gore, I really can't stay and more.

I'm covered in sweat, and you haven't come yet—
My God! It's a quarter to four!'

'At least you don't have that problem,' he added, smugly. 'I can always make you come. A most superior skill.'

'Yes,' said Ejaculata, drily. 'But if you want another one yourself, get my man into Pop. Okay?'

'I don't want to come again today,' he said, still smug. 'I—'

'Who said today, Rupe, who said today? And who said Gregor, either?'

When it was explained who the candidate was in fact – not the twisted little cockroach but the loaded fantasist – Rupert got much more relaxed. De Salmon-Paste was one of the chosen ones, Eton material from face to foreskin, truly authentic. Utterly despicable, entirely talentless, but with impeccable connexions.

It would not be a piece of piss by any means – but it was more than doable. His Ejaculata days were here to stay.

So getting Horus into Pop was put in train, and after not much longer it was done. It cost a bit of blackmail, and it cost a fair amount of manipulation of the dames. They were a mafia, naturally, and Jackie was a natural mafiosa. She'd been to bed with Matron three times, for starters, which was powerful indeed. Matron was entirely asexual, she slept with no one, ever, and was renowned – revered – for it. After the first time she pointed out that if anyone should ever get to know of it Jackie was dead, which sounded fine to Jackie. Kiss and tell was for footballers, celebs, and other low-lifes, while Jackie had her morals and her pride.

The passage into Pop was not merely a matter of screwing the right people, though, nor even bribery, in a place where the meanest was obscenely rich. It was a matter of putting Horus de Peperpott on the path of glory, in a direction ever upward.

But Horus, inevitably, made mistakes.

Number one was a pretty big one. He told Tennisballwallahheadwallahboy, after sex one day, that he was planning to be King of the World, which Tennisballwallahheadwallahboy passed on to everyone. He was half upset by this – 'I told you in strict confidence, darling girl' – but he was also pleased. It would have been a spot conceited to have told people it himself, and this way he could blush and bluster, insist it wasn't true, and paint himself as being humble, as well as having expectations for the future.

Modest expectations, too – and he modestly forgot he'd already told everyone the news himself. He also took the opportunity to 'finish' with the lovely Indian, on the grounds that he was too good for her (being white), and she was a closet lesbian, (or carpet muncher, as he put it amusingly). The fact was it had been a failure, not much better than Gregor's parted pert posterior, and he thought he'd buy one of the kitchen maids next time, someone more vulgar and submissive.

Grateful, too. Tennisballwallahheadwallahboy had been distinctly ungrateful, and ungracious also, about his hetero technique; one might have thought she'd done it for the cash alone. Well, that had backfired on her, hadn't it? Within a week Matron had given her the sack, on information provided by one of the dames. No names no packdrill, but it was Ejaculata.

One had to keep the Eton standards up.

And he got into Pop.

Ten

It was after this that the lessons began in earnest. Gregor undertook the grooming, although he explained at length to his pupil that that word was never to be used.

'It's banned, okay,' he said. 'That's all you need to know, it's banned.'

'But why? It may not be from classical Greek, but it's a perfectly serviceable word.'

'Have you ever heard of Rochdale, sir? No? How about Jimmy Savile?'

Horus's eyes lit up. He'd heard of Jimmy Savile – one of Lady Thatcher's heroes. So what could possibly be wrong with him, then? The cockroach raised despairing eyes.

'It's what you do to horses and young boys,' he said. 'The saintly Savile groomed young boys for the BBC, and paedophiles in Rochdale and a few other nasty little towns spread it out into the female population. With our lot it was boys, though.'

'Our lot?'

'Tory politicians. Well, mainly Tory. There were a few Liberals, come to think of it. And Labour too. Maybe it's a politician thing. They went to public school, they got bathed by nanny every other night, and their mother warned them off girls who might get pregnant. Good sense, really. Girls do get pregnant; it's their badge of natural inferiority.'

'But our mothers got pregnant as well, presumably. I've only been at Eton a few short terms, but no one's told me my mama's a virgin. Am I wrong?'

Goinn shook his head.

'You're going to be a hard one to train, aren't you? You are not wrong, you are not right, but it's all to do with grooming.'

De Peper gave a shriek of genuine excitement.

'Got you! You said grooming. Banned word! I dare you to deny it!'

'I deny it.'

'Pardon? Oh, I'm sorry, that's vulgar, I meant what. I meant what do you say you didn't say, that you deny it? Oh glory this is difficult, it's so much easier in Latin. *Facet, fassomus, facile.* Simple.'

Simpleton, Gregor thought. In any language.

'I did not use grooming, sir, it is not a word I've ever used. I don't wish to contradict you, but you're wrong. I promise you, it's not in my vocabulary.'

'But I heard you.'

'You did not. What you heard was another little lesson from my playbook. Did Churchill ever invite Welsh miners to eat bullets? Of course he did…not. Did the PM say Brexit would be the easiest thing to do in the history of history? Oh no, oh no, oh no. Did he say the NHS was safe with him and his? Did you ever hear of Richard Nixon? No? George Bush? No? Tony Blair? Did you know Trump's father was a nazi and Hitler's grandma was a Jew? Did the word grooming ever pass my lips?'

Silence. From the sunny playing fields of Eton one could faintly hear the screams of little boys. Then a louder scream, and then a shot. A college racehorse had fallen at a practice fence, perhaps, and the guns had had to be deployed. Soon the Windsor Gipsies (Pikeys in the college parlance) would trundle up in their three-tonner and drag away the corpse for rendering. (Or possibly to feed the poor.)

'Well? Did it?'

Another silence; shorter. Then:

'So what you're saying, cockroach, is that the truth is not the truth if it's not accepted as the truth?'

'Nonsense. The truth is sacred, sacrosanct. But in the game of chance, a lie is always trumps. I did not say grooming, did I?'

'I suppose you didn't.'

'Suppose? You just suppose? Think hard, Horus

Paste-Shippam, you're not an oik from 'Arrer or St Paul's, you know. We speak the truth at School. Nothing but the truth.'

'I did not hear you say it, therefore it was not said.'

'But if you had heard me say it?'

'Still not said. Dear friend, that is a most wonderful lesson that you've taught.'

'I never said a word,' the cockroach said. 'We were talking paedophilia, weren't we?'

'We were talking grooming. How a coloured waistcoat and a Pop silk scarf is the *epifone* of the art. The *alphonse and the ohmigod*, if you'll excuse the reference. The highest *nadir* of them all.'

'Your grasp of languages is extraordinary, sir. Where did you learn them, I wonder. Straight from the horse's mouth, perhaps? Or an orifice some distance further back.'

'I don't understand,' said Nicholae. 'Is that *demotic?* It's not a tongue I'm too well up in.'

Not demotic, Goinn thought, but bullshit. He'd never heard it talked so fluently.

Merde de taureau.

Eleven

Beyond telling lies (the truth) and bullshit (modesty), there were many other lessons for Horus de Peperpott to learn from his pet cockroach. After four halves (terms) in school and one in Pop, he was made to realise that he was too *gauche* to be a proper leader of the world, and had to *'pull his socks up'* (classic Eton slang).

He had come through his essential sex lessons – for wads of cash a stream of maids and scrub-girls willingly lent a hand and sometimes more – but before he could get big-headed at his runaway success (from wettest boy in school to top of the Pop-Soc-Poker League) de Peper had to know for sure what sex was *for*. It was during this phase of his schooling that his mentor got the name of 'Doggo.' Which was not to do with bestiality (much), but because he was only ever in the background. Like Galy Gay, his name must not to come into it.

The change occurred when Horus took him as his fag. It was his idea, but Nicholae was certain it was his.

'I hear you want me for a fag,' the cockroach lied. 'But fagging was abolished in this place in 1972, February the eleventh, three fifteen pm. Wasn't it?'

'What?' said de Peperpott. 'Why?'

'Because to make a smaller, poorer, boy your slave was considered not the thing.'

'What? Why? That sounds like creeping socialism to me.'

'More creeping Aids as I remember. The beaks were quite happy to see small boys being beaten, but some of the forfeits were a bit below the belt. And if a fag was expected to take your trousers off, why not your Y-fronts too? And once the pants were off – well, why not? Far too nice a sight for Oppidans to turn a nose up at which, what?'

'The Bigbobs must have been bereft! You mean the fags were not allowed to—'

'By definition, Nicholae. No fags no fucks, to put it at its crudest. That's when the influx of local maids began. If you weren't allowed a healthy boy to do essentials for you, you must have an unhealthy girl.'

'Unhealthy? Was that a rule?'

'Unhealthy in the sense they were from Windsor. Not smart enough to get a job inside the Castle collecting Corgi crap, nor bright enough to serve ale in the pub. But turn up with a change of knickers at the school backdoor, and you were a shoo-in. One change of knickers only was the rule; more than that meant ideas above your station.'

'But did it work, this ban, Gregor? Did fagging waste away?'

'Almost overnight. Third formers walked without a limp for the first time since the time of Queen Victoria, possibly before. The actual start of the practice is not officially recorded, unlike the end.'

De Peperpott was quietly disturbed.

'Damn and blast, then. I wanted you to be my fag, my heart was set on it. What shall I do?'

'What's wrong with the college scrubbers, though?' Gregor was playing devil's advocate. 'Isn't that a bit stuck-up?

'That's the problem, in a blessed nutshell. To stick your thingie up the hole the lord intended can lead to unintended consequences. Although I didn't listen in biology – so embarrassing – I believe it might even lead to...*babies.* Dreadful things like that.'

'I quite like babies,' Goinn lied. Devil's advocate once more.

'But babies are produced by marriage, not shagging Windsor rough! Say for instance that the serving wench you fell upon was beautiful, and sexy beyond imagination, but her father had no silk.'

'Silk?' queried the cockroach. It was a golden rule he lived by – never ask a question if you don't already know the answer. 'What, you mean the stuff his shirts are made of?'

'It means Queen's Counsel, ignoramus, it means he's a QC. If her father were a mere solicitor how could she keep you to the manner born? No country seat or castle, no ten thousand acres!'

The cockroach played another hand. A trump, but well disguised.

'What if I were to have a job, though?'

His mentor looked at him as though he had gone simple. Horus had been born to bluster, to preen and play the aristo, and had practised since his mother had plucked the nipple from his boneless gums, so to speak.

'Don't talk nonsense,' he puffled, like an ocean squall. 'Wash your mouth out with Perrier! Nay, fiddlesticks, with Armagnac and soda! Glenfiddich at a pinch! Where was I?'

'You were talking bollocks,' said the cockroach, meekly. 'You were talking jobs,' he added louder. 'Jobs I might aspire to.'

'But God knows why I bother, eh? Within two short decades this country's been bankrupted by socialism. Prince Andrew can't afford to fly Stateside any more because he can't afford the airfares, and one of his nephews had to marry a blackie, for Christ's sake! We're in the shit, completely fucking fucked. Bloody lebbage lovers. Bloody Labour party.'

Labour, eh, wee Gregor Goinn thought. I must stop looking at Fake News.

'What about banking, sir?' he said. 'Real estate? Letting the tycoons in from Russia and the East has done wonders for the housing market, hasn't it?'

'Indeed it has. But how much capital have you got at your disposal?'

'Capital? What's capital?'

De Peper was in his comfort zone. This insect just had to be his fag!

'Capital is the money you need to buy the real estate,' he said expansively. 'Did you learn nothing about money at St Paul's? Play your cards right and you could end up as Chancellor like young Gideon.'

'But I didn't go to St Paul's. If I was a banker—'

'The money that you had would not be yours, would it?'

'What? But—'

'Well it would be yours in theory, but in fact it's only yours when you've reached the top of the profession. Until then, it actually belongs to the people who put it in your bank and let you use it.'

'What – they can take it back? My money?'

'They can. Their money.'

'But that's not fair!'

'Unless they took it *all* away,' said Nicholae de Peper. 'Leaving your bank destitute. Now *that* would be okay.

That would be champion.'

'But that's ridiculous.'

'The opposite. For if the money went away, all in a lump – there'd be a huge financial crash. A slump. Black Monday, Tuesday, Wednesday, Thursday, you name it.'

'Friday?' Gregor said.

'Indeed – Black Friday's got a lovely ring to it. You've hit it, see – maybe you could be a banker after all. For if there is a crash, the banks get saved, don't they? The government bails them out, gives them everything they need or want. Elegant and sweet.'

'But if it was their fault—'

'The rule of rules is that it's not their fault. Fault's for losers, and they'll get their money back, so they're not losers are they?'

'Get it back how? It can't be that simple, surely?'

'Simpler. The government cut vital infrastructure, cut facilities, cut benefits and wages, police, prisons, fire services, then whatever. *Nobody* loses.'

'Cut HS2? That's a money sink.'

'Don't be ridiculous, that would hurt their friends. Top people need top money, and as it's the bankers' job to build all up again, they'll need to be paid extra, won't they? Plus a knighthood here and there to thank them for their hard work and brilliance.'

'Why not just let them fail, though?'

'You sound like a socialist. They can't fail because

they can't fail, can they? Countries would smirk behind their hands at us, England would be a laughing stock. Their remunerations must *increase,* in gratitude for saving the economy. And the faces of the politicians.'

'And the politicians' role in all of this?' Gregor Goinn asked. 'I think you'll have to tell me that.'

'They protect the ones who run the show, the faceless ones. The ones who live in this country to make the wheels go round, but pay no taxes because their money is offshore. Britain once had an empire, can you believe that? We stole India off the Indians, Africa off the Africans, and little bits and bobs off all the little bits and bobbers. When it all went down the pan we kept some cut-price real estate, mainly islands in the Caribbean – and called them tax havens. They store money for the deserving rich, for a quid or two a year, and the cash rolls in. Everybody gains except for the exchequer, which is us. FGB. Formerly Great Britain.'

'And the deserving rich—'

'Is me. Not you lot, me lot. Lords of the Universe. Eton boys.'

'But I—'

'Got here because a Beak took pity on your… No, that is scurrilous. Let's just say a pretty little dame, shall we? Who shall be nameless.'

He looked at the cockroach with the infinite superiority of breeding, and Gregor smiled back humbly. Well, adoringly, as Horus saw it. If he only could have known young Goinn's thoughts…

'And the smartest trick of all,' he said, 'the masterstroke of the British Empire, was inventing Royalty. Not theirs, ours. They might have had a few fuzzywuzzy Clowns-in-Crowns in what they call their heritage, but we had Elizabeth our Queen and her consort jester Phil the Greek, so fireproof he can call them what they really are. Picaninnies with watermelon smiles, slit-eyed Chinkies, jungle-bunnies, oh he's done wonders for our self-esteem. Just don't let him drive you home!'

He was in the fullness of his pomp, and Gregor Goinn watched with joy. This prat was oven-ready for his role, self-love was blazing from his piggy eyes. The cockroach had a sudden inspiration: the fatboy's hair was much too short. Those eyes would look sincerer through a tousled curly mop to hide their vacancy; a glow of *faux* naivety. Women would die for it; they'd spontaneously lactate.

At last his goal was clear before him. Henry Higgins to a halfwit Julie Andrews. He'd wear gorblimey trousers and sell off council flats.

As so often when de Peperpott excelled himself in rhetoric, he achieved a minor trouser bulge. He grabbed it frantically, and his coefficient sonority rose like a Goodman's woofer. He was in the spaffing zone!

'And to put the tin lid right upon it,' he perorated

further, 'we gifted these supporating shitholes that we conquered the full panoply of English law. A native who spots a sweet white naked titty, even by the merest accident – can be hanged! The Queen alone has power to reprieve, and she won't in case the Lords make her start paying taxes for being soft. Neat.'

'You mean the Royal Family don't pay tax? Isn't that a fiscal waste?'

'Never over-milk a milch cow, Goinn, you must be much more subtle. Prince Charles, for instance, is the Prince of Wales, which means that he owns Cornwall of all places, so all the farmers and the fishermen are his tenants. And they're proud to doff their caps and pay him for the privilege, naturally.'

'Fucking hell,' said the disingenuous cockroach, perhaps a little coarsely. 'How did he get that gig? Lucky Chuckie!'

'Lucky my arse, he stole it, didn't he? Not personally, he's too much of a tit for that, he went to Gordonstoun like his pizza-paedo son Prince Andrew. The Royal Family got there in the first place through force of arms, and they stay there by the stupidity of their loyal subjects. Piece of piss.'

Nicholae de Peperpott Paste-Salmon (or vice versa) took a breath so deep his bumhole almost burst.

'And to have you as my fag will be a piece of piss also,' he said. 'You're such a nasty, scruffy misshaped wee homunculid I'll call you Doggo, and together we'll go far. You'll be my amanuensis, which is a Greek word I learned off Phil himself. It's classical.'

'I'm honoured,' said the cockroach. 'Why Doggo though?'

'I want you in the darkness. You're too ugly to be seen. I want you always in the background. Lying.'

Good call, thought Grigori Goinn, I'll lie anywhere. Consider me your right hand man, Horus Borus. Your right hand man and power.

Behind the throne.

Twelve

There is another club in Eton, and when de Peperpott had sucked full measure of self-confidence from the teachings of his bumboy (as the nastier elements of this club called Gregor) he aspired to join it too. To be in Pop was fine for starters, but with money and a twisted brain behind him, his ambition was much higher. From being black-balled to begin with, he'd shot up the ranks to President, one single act of sporting prowess securing him top spot.

This came during the annual game between Eton and their sporting rivals, Arrer in the 'ill. A deeply inferior establishment, founded only in the nineteenth century, and mocked constantly by its betters, it played better ball games far better than its betters did, and mocked the Wall Game as a breeding ground for thugs and hooligans and prime ministers.

This would not have hurt so much had the annual game of rugby – named after another inferior establishment, Rugby – not ended always in humiliation for the

Windsor Wonders. In 1931 the Arrers licked them 97-0, and a grudge match during the Blitz would have been even worse had a stray bomb not killed seven of their players, allowing School to fight back to a draw.

Of all the stalwarts of the Wall Game young Horus Nicholae was strangely the best, because his bribes were exemplary, and the fatness of his belly meant he bounced whenever barged. He weighed enough to make opposition forward moves impossible also, and stood post-match drink and sex parties for both sides. No wonder he was President of Pop.

For the Arrer match in question, then, he was persuaded to fly the flag for Eton, on the grounds the opposition was fielding an unfairly robust fifteen. This advantage was offset by the fact that the home team were seventeen years old and the opposition just eleven, but by half-time School was fading fast.

After lemon halves and pep talk from the Sporty Beak, the Eton men rushed out in better heart. Each man was told which opposition child to mark and 'mark him good.' Nicholae's target was the smallest and the fastest, and it had been drummed into him how dangerous he was.

For the honour of the school, thought Horus, as the wee opposition bug shot across his gaze, ball under arm, eyes firmly on the touch-line, speed unassailable. But he was only half the weight that hit him, and the de Pepergrinder knees sank deep into the little Arrer stomach.

'Shit and corruption,' Horus told his anxious teammates when the hearse had gone. 'I got a really nasty scratch. Grease-Blobbe's Alma went down on me and kissed it better.'

School won for once, however, because the referee (Sporty Beak's same sex husband; how modern Eton was these days!) disallowed the try on the grounds that corpses weren't allowed to score, however fresh they were. And in the gang bath afterwards, Nicholae felt first a warm tongue slide into his ear, and then a sexy whisper.

'Bullingdon Club tonight,' it said. 'Five to eleven. Bring money. Liquor. Lots of tissues. I might be able to sneak you in.'

For once, Horus de Peperpott thought very fast. *Multo smartish*, to use the vernacular of Plautus.

'Can I bring my little pet?'

'Who?'

'Doggo. He's—'

The tongue slipped from his ear. The voice was harsh.

'Fuck off. Or as they say in the languages you're so fond of – no.'

'Oh. Ah. I—'

'Fist me the fucking soap, you poof.'

And that was the end of that.

Thirteen

It was not, of course. There's no end of what can't be smoothed over in the bathtub with a bar of soap. But more importantly, the Bullingdon Club was nothing at all to do with Eton School in theory, and Doggo warned Horus in no uncertain terms not to touch it with a bargepole.

'What do you mean they want you in?' he said. 'It's a gang of Oxford Uni rich gits with literally more money than sense. The joining fee's so high it's never appeared in print, and the uniform alone costs four plus grand.'

'Uniform?' said de Peper. 'I wouldn't want to be in a club that wears a uniform.'

'Except Pop, of course. But I suppose that's different?'

'Well naturally it's different. No one else in Pop's got a scarf as fine as mine, have they? And the embroidery on my underpants is unmatched.'

'Not that a Popper's meant to flash his understrappers. It's a sacred thing between a man and wife. Like skidmarks.'

'But you said I mustn't have a wife.'

Doggo shook a weary head. Pygmalion would have screamed at such stupidity in his own fair lady.

'I said no such thing. I said not to fuck the maids or dames or even Matron because of pregnancy. Don't you ever listen?'

'Matron, is it? Oh bloody hell, Dog, that's a bridge too far!'

'Also a joke. Matron would eat you up and spit the pips out. And Matron don't get pregnant. She infibulates.'

'Gosh. You mean tells lies about it?'

'Shut up and turn your brain on. Sex is dangerous because it leads to babies, and babies lead to broken homes and poverty. Marriage, to an Eton man, is for two things only – money and position. And don't tell me you've got enough already. Cash, that is.'

'I'm not exactly poor, though. Ma and Pater—'

'I've told you this before: fuck ma and pater. Until they croak, the money's theirs. And you've got siblings. They'll want some too. You need it now, and you need lots and lots and lots. And as for titles…'

'When the old man dies I get to be—'

'A member of the House of Lords. Three hundred measly quid a day, and they make you sign for it, for fucksake. You have to turn up, even if it only takes two minutes to make your mark and go. How demeaning's that? As an Englishman you'd rather die, I hope.'

Fifteen hundred quid a week to do fuck all, Horus thought. Doggo was right. Pin money.

'Good,' he said. 'Explain no marriage then.'

'I didn't say no marriage. Marriage is essential, vital. It's absolutely something you must do.'

'You've lost me now, mate. Why?'

'A title, land, inheritance, a dowry – need I go on?'

'I thought those things were in the past. I thought they'd faded out.'

The cockroach rolled his tiny eyes.

'On the contrary, they make the world go round,' he said. 'Three boys in the sixth got engaged last year to a cool eight million, and half the Virgin Islands. And don't call me mate, it's low. Raise your eyes above a scrubber's hemline to a father's trouser bulge, wallet department. Got that?'

'Yes sir.'

'And don't call me sir. People will think we're in love.'

Doggo knew how to turn a joke, and Horus appreciated his generosity. He no longer knew what he'd do without this strange lad now, his fag and mentor. In a way he thought he did sort of love him. Oh God; the Eton sickness.

'But you still look like a cockroach though,' he said

robustly. 'You're still a gimpy, limpy creep. Tell me about the Bullingdon. Can't Etons really not be in?'

Doggo laughed.

'Well those who go to Oxford can,' he said. 'Which is all of us who want to, obviously. But it's like Pop, you need an invitation. They wake you up in the middle of the night and smash your room and your belongings up. And chuck your booze away. And blow your condoms up with hydrogen and float them through the window to the quad.'

De Peper did not know how to use a condom, but dared not say so.

'Then in the evening, afterwards,' Goinn continued. 'That's when the fun begins. They take you on a jaunt all over Oxford. You've got to be half pissed before you start, and by the time you've smashed your first shop window, you've got to be certified as completely arseholed.'

'Certified? You must be joking. Who the hell would sign it?'

'Any Oxford doctor, obviously. Who didn't want it put around he felt up lady patients for a laugh. One GP who refused was bombarded with so many complaints of inappropriate touching he got struck off and then committed suicide. Nice chap.'

'And did he touch up female patients?'

'Doubt it, he was gay. Or as the Bullers say, a raving,

screaming, knob-gobbling fairy queen.'

'Bullers?'

'Oh come on, Horus, don't pretend you're dumber than you are. We've had prime ministers who still greet old club mates in the street with "bullerbullerbuller". I'd name them for you except for loyalty to the school; Dave Cameron.'

Later on in life, after his own initiation, Nicholae de Peper smuggled the cockroach on an expedition as 'observer,' and it was a classic. Eleven Bullers, dressed to the nines in longtail suits with white silk facings, went marching down their chosen street – chosen to be full of plebs and grockles, wives with babies, old men and women unsteady on their zimmer frames – and shouted demotic phrases, which they knew were ultra cool, into every passing face.

'Wanker! Bum bandit! Scrotum face! Saggy tits!'

As they swelled up with their brilliance, Gregor Goinn trailed silent in their wake, marvelling at their ineptitude. New leaders of the universe, who were not worth a pinch of shit. How could he mould them into the force for power that he dreamed about?

They had women waiting for them at their chosen restaurant, but women of a certain local sort. Nice girls down on their luck, perhaps, nice girls fed up with lads who worked at Cowley and talked of twin-choke carbs instead of more attractive things, like weddings, children, Princess Di, or sex. A few of them had gone into the restaurant early, by arrangement with the management, and were dressed like French maids, respectable and demure. But beneath each *jupe de bonne* nothing but a nice vagina, shaven or furry, to suit any taste.

The Buller boys were all well oiled when they entered the arena for the evening, some so far on that they could hardly stand. There were customers in already, and they were horrified by this onrush of young men in morning dress.

'Bullerbullerbuller!' the yell went up, and a young blood called Oik Osbore (no relation) grabbed at what he assumed was a hired prostitute, tore her dress down to the waist, then lunged forward and threw up on her rather nice bare breasts.

She screamed, her husband made to punch Oik in the face, and two more of the gang laid him spark out on the floor with a champagne bottle to each temple (*brut, bien sur*). It could have turned quite nasty, but the Bullingdons are well versed in such minor *contretemps* and their team of selected heavies moved in smoothly with a stretcher and wads of notes (fifties and above) to calm things down.

'I say, you plebbie fuckers!' de Peperpott boomed out. 'This is a private function, doncherknow. If you're not back to your rathole hovels in two minutes flat the SS will come in! *Raus! Schnell!*'

At which a neat blonde woman, four-square and determined, faced up to Horus Nicholae.

'Assuming you're the *Führer* of zis rabble,' she told him calmly, 'I would ask you to call zem off. You are letting down ze reputation of your *Vaterland.*'

He rose to the occasion like a true blue Brit.

'Farterland?' he shouted. 'Did you say *farter,* grandma? We don't like farters in our country, we don't like foreigners at all. Bullers – give the old Kraut crone the noble Eton chorus!'

It made a Wall Game chant seem feeble. Full-throated and hot it burst up from their straining bellies.

'Two World Wars and one World Cup, doodah, doodah! Two World Wars and one World Cup, doodah doodah day! Hip hip hip! Hoorah hoorah hoorah!'

A young man said quietly to the woman, *'Komm, Mutti. Hier ist nur Scheisse.'*

'*Mutti!*' shouted Horus. 'Is that your fucking mum, you fucking squarehead? Or is it your pissing granny?'

Mutti smiled. She'd come to England because she admired it so much. *Mein Gott*, she thought. Time to have a rethink, *vielleicht*.

'What's your name, you ugly bitch? Don't lie to me, I speak German fluently. And half a dozen other languages. I'm going to be the King, *der Koenigin*!'

'Interesting. But never mind my name,' Frau Merkel said. 'It's immaterial.'

'Don't tell her your name, Pike!' he hooted. 'You wouldn't get that, Krauty, it's a joke. You Germans do not have *ein sense from humour*. Do you?'

'We do in fact,' she said. 'But as Mark Twain once said, it is no laughing matter. Goodbye, *böse Bube*. I trust we never meet again.'

Before he could think of a good retort beyond '*Sieg heil!*' two more Bullers threw up on the carpet, and the hired girls came in. Topless, bottomless, legless, you name it. As the restaurant emptied, the noise level went ballistic, as the prostitutes summoned up wild empty laughter to hide their desolation.

That's what the cockroach thought, in any case, and it made him think back to his mother, and the hard life she had had to help him on his way. What an idiot, he thought, she was no better than a scrubber herself. He hated prostitutes and prostitution, and would sacrifice anyone and anything to rise above all that.

Come to think of it, his mother was starting to rock the boat at Eton, she was slipping her safe moorings, notice had been taken. He might, when push moved on to shove, have to think about her future. Mama, he thought – your days are maybe numbered.

But in the meantime there was much to watch and wonder at. Vulvae, both bestubbled and hirsute, were being flashed all round the table, which was groaning under the weight of legs of lamb and lithe loose limbs. He recognised a buttock as de Peperpott's from Wee Jock Vaine-Govey's toothmarks, and watched a dirty digit slide up the grotty gulf until engulfed. Good normal wholesome sex, Bullingdon Club fashion. Truly there was nothing in the world to touch it.

Gregor Goinn sighed. This really was the road to hell. On the way back to Eton College, they trashed five more cars, smashed a stained glass window, and overturned an invalid carriage (sadly empty) outside a doctor's surgery. Then they rang 999 to report a 'vile outbreak of vandalism, probably by blacks or Muslims', vandalised the phone box for good luck, and stoned the prowl car the plods sent out.

On a global scale, he thought, this could be his pathway and his goal. Disrupt, destroy, delude, deliver.

And always in the background, always hidden. Horus Nicholae de Peperpott Paste-Shippam could be the frontman. While he was Lying Doggo.

Fourteen

'So what did you think of it? As a night out? Did it live up to expectations?'

'Class!' replied de Peperpott. 'I thought the girl-on-girl climax to the show was the bestest thing I ever saw. Three colours, eh – black, white and khaki. And I'd have had all three of them if Grease-Blobbe hadn't pointed out that racial minorities are riddled with syphilis, the dirty bastards. It was fun to stick Mack Hustings up them in my place, however. Snooty little pill.'

'He did all three,' nodded Gregor judiciously. 'I counted them in and I counted them out again. If we're lucky we'll watch his legs drop off when their Aids kicks in.'

'Isn't that a bit racist, though?'

'I didn't use the N-word, did I? Or the P for that matter. Just watch those words and everything's hunky dory. You've got to call a spade a spade, though, otherwise what's the point of being the master race? Next you'll be saying we shouldn't call Aids the Poofter

Plague.'

Nicholae was on his bed, covered in a stained sheet. Grease-Blobbe had sent along his nanny after breakfast to administer what she called 'a lick and a promise' to the exhausted warrior. Put lead in his pencil.

'Did you not think it was a bit excessive, though?' the cockroach continued. 'Trashing the police car could have been a step too far. You can't be sure when the rozzers might change sides. They even let Labour voters join the Force these days, I'm told.'

'Rubbish! Pater's a dear friend of the Commissioner, he wouldn't dream of letting scum in. You're not going soft, are you? I can always get another fag, you know.'

'Not getting soft, but urging caution, maybe. The Bullingdons aren't as popular as they used to be, you know – poking your pudding in a porkers' prod-hole can lead to stories in the red-tops. Then there's the compensation. Do you know how much last night's high jinks cost?'

'Not the least idea, nor do I care to. You're coming on all grammar school again, Goinn. I gave Grease-Blobbe's nanny my bank card to pay out what it took. Next you'll be suggesting she can't be trusted, which considering what you watched her do to me just now—'

'Not her that worries me,' said the cockroach. 'I was thinking of the rowdiness. The hooliganism, the hired whores, the vomit in the street, the shouting slag and slapper at that black vicar's wife.'

'Oh come on, Goinn, don't you take a pride in being British? I know you like funny clothes and wearing benny hats and anoraks, but you were born here, weren't you? Your mater's straight down the line, so why can't you be?'

'Straight down the line? Ejaculata?'

'Exactly. An English rose, who shags like one, just push it in and push it up and haul it out and wipe it. Oh, I— Ah, ahem.' He cleared his throat, and made the usual noises that he seemed to think were speech. 'Not that I, of course… Well! Cripes! Rumours, that's all, filthy rumours! And her jolly old sex ring's entirely respectable, only Beaks and Backers can attend. I suppose you knew about that, my little cockroach? Of course you did.'

Better let him have a bit of triumph, Gregor thought.

'Shit,' he said. 'How did that get out? Does anybody else know, or just you?'

'Leaked out would be more like it,' snorted the chubby morsel on the bed, who had thrown back the counterpane and was eyeing Gregor with a strange light in his eyes. 'Just you and me, I promise you. I've never told another soul.'

'And you don't lie, do you?'

'I can honestly say I've never told a lie in all my life,'

said de Peperpott. And God help him, Goinn thought, he believes that that's the truth.

'How much to keep it that way, then?' he said.

'Talk to my people,' came the grand response, 'I don't do trade. My finance man will come up with a price.'

There was naked hunger in his grin. He licked his lips.

'That's me,' the cockroach answered, also smiling. 'I'll get in bed then, shall I? Gosh though, you're insatiable, Alma could hardly walk when you let her go. You're the king of kings of kings.'

'I am, ain't I? And modest with it. Shall I do you doggy fashion? I haven't had a proper poke for days. Woof woof!'

Afterwards (crap, as usual) they talked of power, and how Horus was going to achieve his dream of domination. He would never be a *cruel* dictator, he insisted, he craved only love. Plus subservience. Plus a *droyt de senior* better than anybody's *droyt* in history.

'Race,' he said. 'That's the key to domination in this country, race and greed and poverty. After the barons of the press have showered me with wealth for spreading lies and nonsense and rank prejudice, I'll go into politics. I'll bend the truth to fit my will, and do it with such flair that every time I'm sacked for lying, other men will fight to take me on. To take them in in their turn, to take them for a similar ride.'

'And me?'

'Don't be so conceited, cockroach – you are nothing. I'll go up to Oxbridge and I'll get a double first, I'll leave Pop behind to lead the Bullingdons, I'll impregnate pretty girls *ad lib* and pay them off until I find my one true love to marry, whose father and whose mother will be loaded, titled, and hold the rest of Britain in contempt except the Queen, God bless her.'

'And all who sail in her,' Gregor muttered. 'Perhaps you might consider marrying a spare princess?'

De Peper snorted.

'With Phil the Greek as pa-in-law? I wouldn't fit in, would I? I haven't got a racist bone in my body, and that man's a raving Nazi.'

'He's a Greek.'

'I speak his language then, don't I? And dear old Liz herself's a German, which is the next best thing, although I'd rather die than speak that filthy tongue. If her so-called subjects knew where they all came from they'd go berserk.'

'Is it a secret?'

'It doesn't need to be. The English are the worst-educated people on the world, and the Sun and Mail and Telegraph are there to keep it that way. The press is owned by 'offshore patriots' like the Barclays, Harmsworth and Rupe Murdoch, who don't pay a bean in tax and make Croesus look like a fucking pauper. The richest of the lot is Facebook, which goes to show just what I'm on about. Motto: Do no evil – right! Good old Markie Suckerberg.'

'So you hate them, do you? That surprises me. I'd have thought…'

'Safer not to think with your brainpower, Blob. It would surprise me too if it were true, and I beg you to note the subjective mood, which is proper Greek, unless you think I mean subjunctive, which I don't. It ain't true though, it's the opposite, the *zeugma*. What do you think this school exists for? Come on, spit it out! There'll be questions afterwards.'

Gregor had his own ideas, but he loved to see the halfwit in full flow. He guessed the words 'great' and 'Britain' would come heaving into view. How long to wait?

Not long. Not long at all.

'We come to Eton to achieve great wealth and power,' said de Peperpott. 'Not just for ourselves, that would be selfish, but for our country, Britain, England, the land of great Saint George. Great Britain, remember that great word, and roll it round your loving English lips. Great Britain, cockroach, great, *great,* GREAT! And the way to that is through those other English virtues, wealth and power.'

'And education, sir?'

'Yes, education!' He rolled it out with great sonority. 'Education, education, education, as the man who took Britain into war and lasting bankruptcy lied so stirringly. Great speech in one way, for it put his Party out of power for decades, thanks Tony; but total bollocks in another. What made Britain great, and will again, is one simple thing. Go on!'

'Oh,' said Goinn, pretending he'd been caught on the hop. 'Er? Is it racism?'

'Ah!' said Horus. 'Two then. Racism certainly is one.'

'Greed?'

'Ah, greed. Well, maybe I'll give you that one, too. Yes, greed is good. But—'

'A good, strong, rightwing government? Trump, say. Or Bolsonaro. Erdogan. Victor Orban. Er…'

'Oh come on, you moral midget! *Think*!'

'But Britain's a democracy. Surely the voters—'

'The voters want the thing that made old Britain great! Racism! Greed! Imperial adventures! Subjugation of all lesser peoples!'

'But isn't that what Germany..? I mean Nazism? Adolf Hitler?'

'Adolf Hitler was a fine man spoiled by a little Jewish blood, which he had the good grace to deny. But he had one enormous flaw. Do you not see it? Have you not paid attention to your Beaks?'

Goinn was transfixed. He'd taught his doctrine

more successfully than he'd dared to hope. This chubby blonde Narcissus was almost up with him. As a figurehead, he could lead the way to undreamed of power.

So he pretended not to know. He preferred to hear the answer from the horse's mouth.

'He was *not English!* That was the flaw,' declared the horse. 'Not one of us! Some Germans are all right, I grant you, and they had the right idea, which is why the Royal Family were so close to them before the war. But the pinkos ruined it, they thought Herr Hitler was on the wrong side, and decided we must lick him. They made the eternal liberal mistake of thinking they were so morally superior the Krauts would crumble like Swiss cheese, they'd be full of holes!'

'*Lächerlich,*' said Goinn quietly. 'As you so truly said before.'

'I said *liquorice* but never mind, you'll learn. They thought the Krauts would crumble but Herr Hitler thought another thing, perhaps he had English blood as well as Kike. He damn near rolled us up like a piece of carpet – France, Holland, Belgium, until he was knocking on our door. Then – cometh the hour, cometh the man. Our authentic saviour, Winston Spencer Churchill. Another Eton hero! Another full-blood Englishman.'

His mother was American, thought Grigori, with a Russki shiver of distaste. And he went to 'Arrer, and only scraped in there by skin of teeth and size of daddy's wallet.

'Highly likely, sir,' he said.

'The greatest ever Englishman,' Horus continued. 'All those wondrous milestones that he achieved for us! The Bengal famine – three million fuzzywuzzies dead. Gallipoli – word-beating corpse count. The Tonypandy triumph when English soldiers shot down the unarmed Welsh, the Siege of Sidney Street where Serb scum were locked in and incinerated. "Better to let the house burn down than spend good British lives," the great man said. My God, we need a statue of him on every corner, every street!'

Time to strike, thought Gregor.

'I could see you as another Churchill, easily,' he said. 'With me close up behind, you could—'

'Close behind me fiddlesticks, you oaf, I can do it by myself! I'm brilliant! I'm a genius! I'm invincible!'

'But you need to kill my mother, sir. That is imperative.'

'What! Kill your mother?'

'Oh forgive me, though, you couldn't do it, could you? Not even Alexander the Great killed women.'

'Pshaw! Alexander was the weakest of the Romans! He slept with men! Pass me a tissue, will you, you've let a drop of spunk get on my pillow. Of course I can kill her.'

'People might call you cruel, though. Say that you

were heartless. Mum's crimes were not so very great, maybe.'

De Peperpott puffed out his flabby chest. I'll have to get those titties off him smartish, Doggo thought, or he'll never be able to pose like Putin.

'Well, I think they were great enough for anything,' said Horus. 'Disgusting to the Nth degree. What were they again, just remind me will you?'

'The way she killed poor Rupert, for starters. The way he hanged himself because she told.'

'Told what?' Horus was confused. 'I didn't know poor Rupe was dead, did I? Oh, what bitches women are!'

'Yes, she didn't *have* to put her prices up so drastically, did she? Then spread it all round Windsor he had to find cut-price pleasure screwing lebbage boys? And—'

'Oh glory be! And *what*?'

'Well, lending him the pearl-handled revolver from the Combined Cadet Force cabinet so he could blow his brains out all over the bleeding wall.'

'The Eton wall?'

'Good joke, sir, but it's not a game, you know. I mean, to use the school revolver! This is Eton. We live by honour. This has *tarnished* it. You've got to kill her.'

The face of blubber crumpled.

'But I'll be a murderer! It's against the law!'

'We are the law, Mr Shippam-Paste. And the fountain

of all honour. The Eton motto! *Nole me tangere.'*

'Don't eat my tangerine,' said Horus, automatically. 'Oh never, never, *never* has that motto been so heart-rending.'

He blubbed so hard the tears ran down his tits. And the cockroach played his masterstroke.

'But if it's any trouble, sir – why don't I do it for you?'

What? There was only one honourable response, just one. A horrified refusal. It didn't happen.

'I too have honour, sir,' Gregor continued. 'I am your fag. I am an Eton man myself. And it is thanks to you. All of it.'

Well hardly, Horus Borus thought. But he let that go.

'What,' he blustered. 'You'll kill her for me? Your own mother? Oh God, oh golly gosh, that really is too kind! But I couldn't possibly accept! How will you do it? When?'

'There's only one condition,' Gregor Goinn said. 'No no, don't collapse again, it's hardly onerous! It's just – no questions afterwards, not a single one.'

'From whom?'

'From anyone. It must be as if it never happened. As if Mrs Ejaculata Goinn never existed. Galy Gay again, sir, remember Galy Gay.'

'I do,' lied de Peper, fervently 'Oh I do, I do! No questions, ever. From no one and his dog!'

'As I said before, good joke. And as I also said before, this is not a game. I will need a signed certificate – which I promise you will never see the light of day again – that you did the job yourself. Legal. Incontrovertible. Then I'll take the body in the dead of night to a lonely place in Hampshire called the Devil's Punchbowl, and for your own safety you won't even know when and where I dug the grave. In case they put MI6 on you. And 4 and 5 as well. And torture you.'

Horus De Peperpott went pale.

'They don't do they? The British secret services? Torture you?'

'Not if the price is right. You won't even get a bill that could be used in evidence. A gentleman's agreement. A handshake, Eton style. Suit?'

The gratitude of the naked fat boy was almost overwhelming.

'I tell you what,' the cockroach added. 'I'll have her house as compensation for my trouble. I won't be in her will I'm guessing, even if she made one, but Eton's crawling with lawyers who can sort that out. You'll never see her again, obviously, but if there's anything you want me to give her from you, before I take her to the Punchbowl? A small momentum? Keepsake? Something quicklime proof?'

There wasn't really. Horus Nicholae wasn't even sure he'd ever met her, and guessed he'd not have liked her if he had. But the sentimentality of the thought gave him a needy twitching down below.

'Cripes!' he said, giving it the lightest flick. 'What a way to seal a deal! You really are a very loyal friend.'

What do you know about loyalty, Doggo thought? I'll have your back, though, for the rest of time. And when it comes to it, I'll stick a knife in it, so hard you'll never lie again.

By God, but that would be a hard blow, wouldn't it? It would have to be. To penetrate that mighty carapace of ego.

Hard as fuck.

Fifteen

As the Fat Stooge hadn't noticed that Rupert had both shot and hanged himself, and his disappearance didn't even make a paragraph in Fixtures, the Fat Stooge felt a burden lifted off his neck. The death had cost him dear – a good few thousand squid – but what of that? And tales that the late Dame Cockroach and Rupert were later seen in Cannes alive and well he wrote off as the merest piffle; a cone of it, inverted.

With Goinn lying doggo at his back, he set himself to climb the tree of life. Eton was the place to start, no doubt of that, but there were other mountains he had to scale, with sherpas or without. Lying Doggo began a programme which would take de Peperpott to the zenith of ambition (unless he had been serious about Kingship of the Whole Wide World), with himself lurking in the background, pulling strings.

With the world wagging as it did at this time in history, Essex was not the only way, but had a twin in politics. The two phenomena were sufficiently linked to make the confluence rather satisfactory, and the vulgarity of both satisfied a deep need in Goinn's soul. He loved his mediocrity, his ambition, his immorality, his drive. Humble beginnings (not that his necessarily were) were a tremendous spur, in that each inch up the reptile trail of life gave him the satisfaction of slithering through the dreams of those who thought themselves superior. Those at the apex thought they were there through merit, and knew they could not be toppled from below. Gregor hated them, and pretended he was not one of them. His triumph, that way, was infinitely more sweet.

Humble beginnings became his greatest lie. He forgot about, and then denied, the titles in his family, the estates, the reparations from the ancient slave trade that had enriched and ennobled the Goinn clan. He was prepared, at every school he went to, to claim that he was destitute, and any honours that he won had come from his supreme intelligence and his animal fighting spirit. His mother, who strangely loved him dearly, recognised this weirdness early – and shared it to some weird degree – and got him into Eton through her (unnecessary) dameship and her (innate) guile.

She chose an image for him – some sort of hippy tramp – and modelled his hair and face and bearing after the *louche* model of the famous Russian monk Rasputin, with a touch of Raskolnikov thrown in for extra bottom. She trained him as a child on the great models of the Communist regime, with a blending in of the great amoralists from the far left and far right.

'Not Hitler, though,' she exhorted him. 'Nazis, yes, but the useful ones, the ones with brain not just charisma. In politics, my son, let Goebbels be your shining star. His only mistake was that you can't fool all of the people all of the time. You can; of course you can. You just need a better shill than Adolf Schicklegruber.'

By the time he met his shill at Eton, by the time he became de Peper's fag, the future was mapped out. He had tried and tested all his early friends, and had destroyed them. He lived on bridge and gin, almost never seemed to sleep, and never seemed to work or eat. He inspired his loyal cohorts to break the law with outrageous daring, but was never present when the law fought back, and cut them dead if they cited him as backup to their stories. He had never heard of them.

Strangest of all was his excoriation of elites. Elites were scum, while laws and rules were for the little people. If you wanted to insult him, call him elite. You would only do it once; there would be consequences. He would incite anybody to everything, and the more 'respectable' they were the more they loved it. And the faster he dropped them when they came unstuck.

He was Lying Doggo (always lying, always invisible), and Horus Shippam-Paste was his greatest creation. Ever since Dr Frankenstein invented them, creatures have been unsuccessful, but Doggo's was the great exception. His success was in inverse proportion to his lack of it, and for many years he truly thought (the creature, that is, not the man) that he would one day be King of the World. President of Pop, top man of Bullers, head of the Oxford Union, head of secret societies (un)known to man. (What of the Masons, you might ask. Well don't.)

A charismatic fucker, then, in fucking as in the rest. He swans through everything, shags everything, lines up the prettiest richest titled girl in the university (who fucks off and marries a dustman because she craves respect) boasts of the best First ever in the history of Firsts and gets a third, and is certified as thick as pigshit.

With Doggo behind him however, he bribes and cheats and threatens and bullies his way right to the top. In journalism (not as we know it) he shags everything that breathes, gets paid more per article every time he's sued, and gets sacked every third Thursday of the month. In a rare moment of despair (trying perhaps to remember who his children are) he confesses he's no good at anything, and Gregor Goinn knows his plan has come to fruit at last.

'Politics,' he says. 'You can't do anything, de Peperpott, so politics is the place for you to shine. You'll meet much thicker men than you are, but without your charisma and your great connexions.'

'Charisma?'

'Oh you know that, Horus. Greek for bullshit. Bullshit is British and it's what made this country great. We're the worst governed country in the world, so you'll be right at home and we'll go far.'

'We?'

'You're in charge, and I'm invisible. Unless there's a great epidemic or something unforeseen and it somehow blows my cover. That's all right though. We keep our heads down, deny everything, and lie like fucking Cretans. That's a classical reference, you don't mind me using it I hope? It's a useful thing, education, as long as the masses aren't allowed it.'

'But we've got to get voted in to make it work. We live in a democracy.'

Doggo fell about.

'Yeah, right. You leave that to me, voting is easy, you ask the Donald, the King Across the Water. This country's built on two things, ignorance and racism, and it's what the punters want. The working classes can be made to vote for anything, but the *zeitgeist* is go right, go right, go right.'

That was almost cynical, de Peper thought. He sometimes feared his mentor might be something of a…dictator? A man who could not be trusted with…democracy? But he was wrong. Doggo had not finished.

'Go into politics, my dear friend, and you can change it for the better, can't you?'

'We. I'd like you with me, cockroach. You're—'

'I'm touched. We, then, but my name must not come into it. Remember Wee Jock Vaine-Govey of the Sewers, our very own Third Man. Most of all remember Galy.'

'I do,' de Peper lied. 'What a jolly name. Gay.'

'It's your way to riches and great power,' Doggo continued. 'Go in, reform, get rid of the dead wood, own newspapers and television, destroy the BBC. Cut taxes for the rich, cut benefits for the scroungers, and tell Europe to stick it up their arse. Churchill once told the truth to de Gaulle in no uncertain terms, do you remember that? Because the big-nosed garlic muncher said America and Russia won the war, not us!'

'God, what an outrage, don't you just hate the French! And the Germans, and the Dutch and Spaniards! As for the pifflepaffle Eyeties – Jesus fucking Christ.'

'Another life lesson. It's what we went to Eton for. And we'll choose the cream of Eton to be the mainstays of your Cabinet when I make you the PM.'

'If. Let's not be immodest.'

'You went to Eton. I went to Eton. It is the Eton way.'

'Grease-Blobbe went to Eton. And his father and grandfather too. All his uncles and relations. Ian Fleming, Guy Burgess, Jonathan Aitken, Jeremy Thorpe, all the greatest patriots went there, and not a sexual deviant among them. They ran the country for us, and we will do the same. Hallelujah, you are right – it will truly be a Golden Age!'

Yes, thought Lying Doggo. You will rocket high into the sky and burn and spatter colours in the firmament, and I will take the other route, the underground. But I will also marry into massive riches, and I will have a title which I'll hide.

'It will be an incredible success,' said de Peperpott. 'I will be revered and loved. I will be the greatest Prime Minister Ingerland has ever known. I will have wives and mistresses, I will have a little dog called Dildo, and kids uncountable. I will be immensely, intensely, *amazingly* rich. Gosh, Goinn, I cannot wait to start.'

Doggo cleared his throat. It was his duty to keep things real, he thought.

'They say that all political careers end in failure,' he said. 'Even Churchill's. And Churchill had a great amount of talent.'

'As a classicist,' said Nicholae. 'But not as good a classicist as I. And he went to a most inferior school.'

'And he killed a lot of men. A lot of lot of men. Admittedly of most inferior races.'

'So there you are then. No contest, QED. Churchill was good, but let's say – second rate, shall we? Compared with me.'

'Well I shouldn't be surprised, de Peperpott. He's got a lovely monument as well. I just hope…'

'What?'

'I hope no fucker pulls him off his pedestal.'

That's all.

The end

Covid Lockdowns (and their author)

Jan Needle has had more than fifty books published, as well as stuff for stage and TV, including plays, series, soaps, and serials. Locked down by our modern plague, he embarked on a project of short fictions ranging from the serious to the silly. This one is either very serious, or very silly – you decide.

Covid Number One was Shakespeare – the Truth, which reimagines the noble Bard as a hapless hack on a scurrilous rag called Ye Globe. Shagsper, Shaxpere, Shakespeare (he couldn't really spell his own name apparently) goes careering around seeking dirt on such notables as Hamlet, King Lear, Romeo, Juliet, Macbeth et al. In later capers you may meet Guy the Griller for example, transported from the mean streets of London to far flung planets, or end up in the milder wilds of Wantage, with its twenty seven pigs.

Critical views of Needle:

'Brilliant. I found myself being drawn back into that twilight world again, despite myself. I was grossly entertained and thrilled…a rare talent.' Jimmy Boyle

'Absolutely wonderful' – Willie Rushton

'What's really amazing is how much he seems to know about so many different things.' Tony Parker, New Statesman & Society

'So topical…[Needle] has a sharp underdog's eye.' John McVicar, Time Out

'Compelling, vivid, racy…describes with unnerving prescience just what is going on.' Guardian

'Recalls the golden age of British investigative reporting: hard-hitting, crusading, alarming prescience.' The Times

Books and info:
  Facebook: www.facebook.com/jan.needle1
  Twitter: @janneedle
  My blog: www.janneedle.com
  Email jan.needle@gmail.com
  My Kindle author page: www.amazon.co.uk/Jan-Needle/e/B004LQ8GL4

One day, who knows, we will have the promised vaccine. In the meantime, a short review would help both my self esteem (also up to you) and my bank balance.
  Read on for a taster of a much different sort of humour!

SHAKESPEARE
THE TRUTH

A memoir

"I would never, ever tell a lie, my liege. Straight up."

Iago (Ensign to General Othello)

Folio ye Firste

Countrie Matters

It was a combination of boredom and an outbreak of the plague virus (Corbyn 19) that made Bill Shagsper move to London. That and the fact his darling wife announced she'd fallen sick with her normal woman's virus one more time.

'But you can't have! God's bollox, Anne, you haven't let me near you for three months!'

'That's it then,' she responded tartly. 'I'm three months gone. Exactly. And it's going to be a boy called Hamlet. Or a girl called Judith, he hasn't made his mind up yet.'

'Decisions always were his problem, weren't they? That's how Denmark became part of Normandy. Or do I mean Norfolk?'

The acid in his voice was biting.

'William,' she said,' that is precisely why you'll never be a writer. Enough with the puns, already! Enough,

enough, enough!'

'Tautology,' he started. 'How many times have I told you not—'

The Le Creuset skillet caught him on the temple, and Shagsper squeaked. But it made his mind up, once and for all.

'Right! I'm off! I've had enough!' he said. 'Domestic violence is meant to be a city thing, but I won't get beaten half so much in London, I'll put money on it. And what I get in groats down here they'll match in golden guineas up in Fleete Streete. Then you'll realise what a star you've lost!'

'Star *mein tukhess*,' snapped back Ms Hathaway, who had a surprising grasp of Yiddish for a country lass from the midlands of merry Ingerland. 'The only Fleete you'll end up in will be ye Ditch, mate. The streete needs talent – and you had the echtomy last year in case you've forgotten. Even the local rag made you take a pay cut, *nicht wahr?*'

Mistress H could be extremely cutting, and to tell the truth Will had little chance of getting back at her. He was too nice was how he saw it, and as 'soft as shite' as his father said. Too soft to even follow him into the gloving trade; he cried fingering even the gentlest kid.

Too soft – worst thing of all – to have seen through Anne H's ploy of telling him she was *up ye duffe* the first time she stole a kiss off him and slipped a bit of tongue into his resisting mouth. Oh that tongue! Oh that feeling! He had thrown himself onto the sward with a paroxysm of nausea, and she had pulled her skirts above her head in a fluid gesture and lain upon him in full view of all the farmers and their hands.

Their hands. Their hands were everywhere as they all joined in – maids and men, nobody gave a jot – and introduced poor bookish Will to what were known around these parts as country matters. They plied him with sack and cider to the bargain, and to this day he had no idea if he'd even done the act itself. Beast with two backs? Beast with up to twenty was more like it. *'Tis dark'* (as the great poet later put it) *'and lurks the naughty deed.'*

Except it wasn't even dark, and there was very little lurking about it. Not much naughtiness either, according to his country cousins, who seemed quite used to this sort of thing.

But Will Shagsper wasn't, and for all he knew he was still a virgin at the end of it. Two days later, though, Ms Hathaway turned up with her father and her mother and announced that she was 'great with child.'

'First time, too!' crowed her mother. 'Until you so cruelly debauched her, Master Shag, my pretty little innocent had never ever lain with man.'

'Despite she's nearly twenty seven, which makes

it ten times worse!' her father said. 'How old are you, you smooth-talking seducer you? You lothario, lounge lizard, you rampant creature of the demi-monde.'

'Now now, pa,' Anne put in blushingly. 'There's no need for potty talk. Mum – tell him.'

'How old, though?' insisted Mr H. He clenched a fist as if to strike Will, who uttered a girlish cry. 'How old? Thirty? Forty? Fifty?'

'Oh no,' cried his better half, her features graunched with horror. 'Not *fifty?* Oh dear God, NO!!!'

'I'm seventeen,' said Will. 'Nearly eighteen, actually.'

'Quite old enough to marry,' said Mr Hathaway. 'Well, thank the lord for that. We'll need some money too, of course.'

'But surely the maiden's parents…' Will muttered, and the fist-in-law was raised much higher. 'No, no, of course. I'm misremembering. Yes, money. The bride price. Yes.'

'Who said she was a maiden, anyway?' said the mother. 'You'll find her worth it, Master S. She's got more skills than being good in bed, she can keel a pot as well as any greasy Joan you'll ever meet. For a virgin she's been very well brought up.'

'Thanks to you, ma,' Annie said. 'You taught me everything I know. Ooh, I feel a little sickly. Could it be the baby's coming now?'

'More than likely,' said her father. 'Shagsper, come

down to the church with me, we'll post the banns and slip the Vic a crafty quid or two. Yes, Anne, you do look pale. We'd better get this done and dusted by the end of Micklemiss, hadn't us?'

'Yes Dad. When's Micklemiss?'

None of them knew, but what of that? The deed was done, Anne Hathaway became an honest woman, and five and a half months later the Shagspers had their bonny bouncing first-born babe. Full term, too. Not a blemish!

It was not the first of many, though – Anne didn't care much for that sort of thing once she'd got the gold band on her digit. Just the odd once or twice when the ale was flowing free, or when Will was not at home in Stratford.

It was not an exactly happy marriage.

Two

A married man, Will Shagsper quickly learned, had to earn a proper living. No good at gloving, as Mr H told everyone in the neighbourhood, not good at anything at all if you asked his wife – within the sheets or out.

'He's like an octopus that's lost an arm or two,' she told her best friend, Gossip Gertrude. 'How many does an octopus have anyway?'

'Just the none, but good long legs,' said Gertrude. 'And their eggs! Would feed an army an ostrich egg would. Oh, octopus. What's one of those when it's at home?'

'I suppose we could ask Will,' said Anne, resentfully, patting her growing belly. 'If he knows nothing else he knows things no other bugger knows nothing about, Gertrude.'

And rude Gert smirked, 'Like putting things in holes. Babies don't grow on trees do they?'

'He thinks they do,' said Anne. 'First time I gave him a hand in bed he thought that I was milking him to feed the baby! He's a jackanapes.'

'Gross,' said Gertie. 'But you're Mrs Shagsper now, ain't you? Your salad days are over, duck.'

'Don't call me duck, it's low.'

'We're in the Midlands duck, get used to it. You're Mrs S that's all there is about it. Sorry.'

'You bloody will be, duck. I'm Hathaway, and that's an end to it.'

'But you're married to him! *Ain't* you?'

'Yeah, okay, alright, I must admit it. But a Shagsper I will never be, my friend. Shagsper. *Shagsper!* What sort of effin name is that?'

'But—'

'And he hasn't got a job except for low-paid scribbling, and he hasn't got no prospects, and he's almost young enough to be my bleedin' *son*. If it hadn't been for them three witches I wouldn't have touched him with a ten foot pole.'

'Three witches? What three witches?'

'That week in Scotland on the charabang. I got pissed one night and I met them at the crossroads. They said they'd tell me fortune for a groat.'

'Bloody Ada, you *were* drunk, weren't you? What did they say?'

'I asked them where the lads hung out, up Scotland way. Where I could get a crafty peep behind the sporran. They went on and on and on.'

'Weird sisters do, it's how they earn their brass. You

wouldn't cough up much if they just said it'd be fine on Tuesday, maybe a spot of rain, would you? Bangs for bucks, that's what it's all about. Talking of which, I spose they told you to get one up you, quick? Get laid, get wed, and no more dreary trips to sunny Scotland (not).'

'I told you, they were kayleyed. They just went on and on about bats' toes and newt's eyes and stuff like that. And trouble; not once but many times. Double trouble, in fact, double double toylen trouble. What's a toylen? Is it a Scotch lavvie sort of thing?'

'Dunno, me duck, has it got a wooden seat? It's dead poetic though, I can see why you were swayed. Toylen trouble. *Double* toylen trouble. Gee widdikins, it's enough to part the thighs of any maid. Not that you were one, natch. Sorry about that, Anne.'

'I'll have you know I was a maid till at least nearly eleven. But it wasn't the toylen stuff in any case. After the lips and noses they got really mucky. I can't remember the details, because my head was in a whirl, but they went on about potions that would bring you to the highest heights. God, Gert, it was so *cool!*'

'Go on! Go on go on go on!'

'Fingers three of birth-strangled babe, can you believe it!? Ditch delivered by a bleeding *drab!* Oh Gertie, Gertrude, Gert. I dived in amongst a bunch of lads almost the moment I got off the chara back home in

Stratford, and it was *heaven!* Every day for a week or more, a fortnight, the whole of harvest as it happened. And the lads wore britches not skirts like them Scotch gits, it was *respectable*. I mean, when you lift a skirt up you don't expect to see a rampant todger, it's not natural. It almost puts you off.'

'Oh Anne, I can't stand the excitement! And I suppose Wee Willie Shagsper had the biggest, did he? Or was it just the straightest one, like King Richard's back before the scoliosis got it? A giant scrotal sack of silk and satin? And you fell in overwhelming *LURVE!*'

'Well,' Anne answered, 'he was *there*, that much I can confirm. Ripeness is all, the man once said, and Wee Willie Dumbnuts was like a medlar dropping off a tree. He was the rawest cony you could ever hope to catch, so I picked myself out of the crush and caught him. I was pregnant.'

'Just like that.'

'Exactly just like that.'

'And you knew he was the father.'

'He had to be.'

'Well someone had to be.'

'Precisely. And all he needed was the ring to slip upon my finger.'

'Important that. Mellifluous. Poetry.'

'Aye. Double, double toil and trouble, fire burn and cauldron bubble, what present uncle, balls my liege, and another glass of sack. To sex and violence, Gertrude.'

'I'll drink to that! You hath a way with words.'

'With young men, too, although he doesn't know it yet. But he's going to change his name, and he's going to find proper employment for the pointy thing he carries in his britches.'

'His Johnson?'

'His quill. He got an education off his father, the only sensible thing that old fool ever did, and I had a quiet meeting with the wight that owns the local rag – well, not that quiet, truth to tell – and my William's dosh shot up a bit like he did. He ranges far and wide all the way up to Birmingham and the Black Country now, doing what he calls his little paragraphs. Dull as ditchwater and the pay's still not that good, but it keeps him out of my bed, big style. He's the Ideal Husband.'

'You mean he comes and goes.'

'He doesn't come at all. Just goes. Gertrude; it is wedded bliss.'

Three

There are worse things in life than jobs and wives, and England in those days was rather prone to plagues. Not pleasant English plagues, but nasty foreign ones brought in on ships my nasty foreign rats.

The most famous outbreak to ever come ashore landed at a sleepy little resort called Brighthelmstone, where princes disport themselves with *ye lusty slappers* of nearby Hove, noted for loose drawers and looser morals. Rated a mere epi-demic at first, it was promoted after a few hundred thousand deaths to 'pan-demic' status, because it was spread by Chinese restaurants that didn't have a wok.

Recurring bouts of Corbyn were quite unpopular with the locals as you might imagine, although they did bump up church attendance as far away as places like Stratford, where preachers with an eye on the main chance could hone up their skills. Unpopular with those who died, but for young men searching for excuses to leave home these outbreaks could be magic.

Bill Shagsper, married, mocked, and mumbled at

by toothless hags, had had it up to here with the daily grind of 'hatches, matches and dispatches' when the latest bout came shooting up country to wreak havoc. He'd sent many job applications to the London journals and been rebuffed, but when two Stratford colleagues died in quick succession and the editor offered him 'a step up for a little token pay-cut,' mild young Willie Shagsper saw crimson red.

'A step up to what?' he shouted (to general astonishment; Bill Shagsper did not shout). 'Beetroot correspondent on half the salary? Swedes! Leeks! Asparagus! What do you take me for? I want to be a superstar! Range far and wide and write on many subjects! *Any* subject beneath the shining sun! My name will be on everybody's lips! I'm going to be a *somebody*!'

His colleagues were all open-mouthed.

'A nobody you mean,' they chorused. 'Zounds, Shaggers, what have you ever done? Your greatest triumph was to ride the village bike up to the altar, and even she made you pay above the odds. You go to London – if you can find it – and you'll end up in the gutter in less time than it takes to tell. Your name will be forgot in Stratford, and no one will ever hear of it elsewhere. Change your mind, lad, while you've got the chance.'

'Good advice,' said the editor. 'Eat humble pie and I'll let you have your job back. What dost thou sayest?'

'Well,' said Shagsper. The reality of what he'd done

was beginning to hit home. His turn to cook the dinner, and Anne would bloody slaughter him.

'Well, sir,' he said. 'I—'

But the editor fell about. As did all his colleagues, even those whose buboes had begun to burst.

'That's a jest, Bill! Can't you tell? God's cods, you wee maid's buttocktrumpet, I wouldn't take you back again at even half the pay! A quarter! Three eighths of two fifths of bugger all! Begone, you cullion. Pisse off out of it!'

Later that same day, his bum still sore from his friends' repeated kickings, his legs aching from the office boneshaker he'd purloined, Will Shagsper settled in a ditch to have a rest and think.

All in all, and despite what had been said and done to him, he was quite chipper about how it had all gone. He was free! Free from the plague outbreak, free from the grotty little town of Stratford, free of Anne Hathaway and her unfunny little ways.

His wage as well, ditto his kids, but what the hell? They'd probably get the virus anyway, and if they wanted, they could come and visit in his swish new London pad. Most probably he'd never see the whole boiling of them again, though. *Prima!*

When he'd decided to make it in the city – bright lights and brothels, as Mrs H had put it snootily – he'd been looking for a change. Life in the fast-lane. Pubs that weren't all called the Ruptured Heifer or the Gutted Goose. Public hangings, and maids who thought (apparently) sex *after* marriage was a bore.

And stories. Oh, he could not *wait* to write those stories.

He'd show the lot of them. Little Bill of Stratford was going to be one great big noise. His name would be in lights…

To pursue the hapless hack further, go here:
https://www.amazon.co.uk/dp/B088NC2Q77

Printed in Great Britain
by Amazon